I0784005

Library of Congress Control Number: 2025914947
ISBN: 979-8-9875917-4-1

Book & cover design: Jennifer Sumeracki, Sumo Design
Editor: Alexa Nussio

Manufactured in the United States of America

Other Editions:
Wolf of My Heart: Originally published in the limited edition of the Hearts,
Panties, and Magic Anthology released by GDRW in October, 2023.
Solstice In New York: New Release, 2025
The Jinni's Wish: Originally published in Power of Four –
Library 1 in December, 2021 (original copyright 2019)

Publisher: Saraybooks LLC

SHIFTERS IN NEW YORK

SHIFTERS IN NEW YORK

COLLECTION

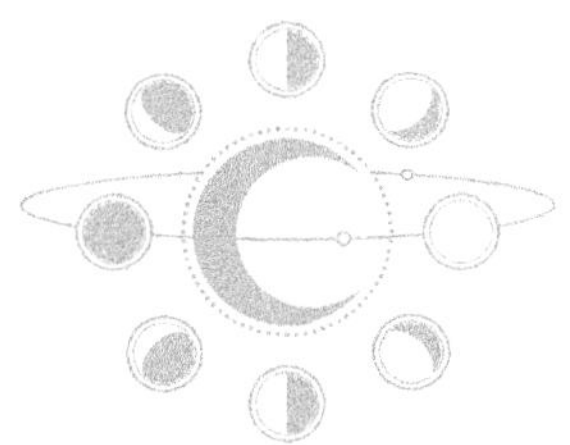

D.A. HENNEMAN

To Brooke Fisher
Remember that story you were reading
on page 48 about "some werewolf
getting it on with a hot elf chick?"
I finally wrote it. It seems we
aren't done with Wisteria...

WOLF
OF MY
HEART

*Can true love find those
who don't want to be found?*

After a full moon and another blackout, a werewolf
finds a mysterious pair of panties in his bed.
Curious about their origin, they lead him to a
New York lingerie store run by a curvy elf.
Now the confirmed bachelor is in real trouble.

1
SAM

It took him a few seconds to get his bearings. They were happening more frequently…the blackouts. He feared piecing together what he was up to the night before since his arms felt like he had pushed back a speeding train for most of it. As his eyes adjusted, he glanced down at his morning reminder that he needed to do more than write about sex.

"What the fuck is that?" He didn't have time for this. He was on a tight deadline.

Sam Randall's eyes came into focus, as he shook the brain fog from the Super Moon that had blind-sided him the night before. He glanced side to side. To his headboard then down to his feet. The ropes he had tied around his wrists and ankles were shredded, and his mouth felt like he had eaten a bag of cotton balls. His assumption that he had chewed through them and had gone out on some sort of adventure was probably dead right since he was naked as the day he was born, except for the tiny scrap of black lace perched on his impressive hard-on.

He looked back at the panties, unwilling to even touch them since the movement would further aggravate the not-so-sleepy giant wearing them like a cloak. He picked them up with two fingers, feeling the brush against an already sensitive situation and noted the store tag.

"So not worn," he muttered. He pulled in the faintest hint of sage and jasmine. The scent made his heart pause. "Where do I know that from?" He spied a gold tree emblem sewn to the hip and ran his finger over the design. "Tree of life," he mused. "Familiar."

The panties were doing things to his dick he didn't want to deal with, so he marched naked to his kitchen to get a zippered bag. It wasn't until he had secured it that he realized the window to his fire escape was open.

"Shit. What have I been up to?"

The cold shower was the third of the week, and he was glad the moon cycle was coming to an end. He had left his home for New York years ago to avoid this very thing. Why the hell was it happening now? Was it because he was creeping up on the big 4-0? A mid-life crisis thing for shifters? Whatever it was, he needed to get to the bottom of it. It was disrupting his plan for bestseller status, and his agent would be pissed if he postponed the edits on his latest novel a second time.

After double-checking and securing all his windows and looking for any more clues that would help him figure out the case of the mysterious panties, he left his apartment at West 58th Street and followed his nose.

The scent he had picked up on got progressively stronger as he made his way toward Central Park. With each step he took, the earthy fragrance broke through the pungent smells of the city streets and went straight to his groin. What the hell was going on? Thankfully, it was early enough that he was alone on the street, saving him some embarrassment. Actually, not completely alone. He slowed his steps as he came up to a black cat in the dead center of the sidewalk, which showed no signs of budging.

He wasn't a fan; cats weren't high on the list of creatures he got close to. They were unpredictable and conniving, so he typically stayed clear. This one wasn't taking a hint though. Each time he took a step sideways to go around it, it slinked into his space. He paused, and the cat stopped as well, placing her sleek butt on the sidewalk. He made sure the area was clear before giving a warning growl to the sassy feline. It was definitely a she—not only could he tell from the pheromones she wore like perfume, but by the way she tipped her head and cast him a cynical glare. He felt as if he were being chastised. She was practically rolling her emerald-green eyes which perfectly matched the stone hanging from her collar. Strange thing for a cat to be wearing, but maybe the owner was into the mystical stuff he saw witches use back home? People here thought of it as spiritual, New Age, or woo woo. He shook the sense of familiarity as feral cats were commonplace among the homeless the closer to Central Park you traveled. Chances were it lived nearby.

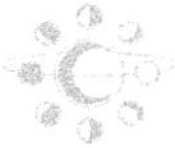

He tried to step over the curb and into the street when she lost her patience. She hissed and swiped at him, effectively pushing him back toward the doorway of the nearest shop. Was this the shop cat? Was it trained to push customers into the store? His nose caught the scent again, so much stronger here. He looked up at the sign perched over the storefront and saw the tree of life image he had seen in his bedroom hours before. He glanced down at the cat one more time before entering the shop. Lucky she had stopped him or he would have walked right past the recessed doorway.

It wasn't until he had taken a few steps into the shop that he realized his mistake. Lingerie. He glanced around, thankful to see other things as well. He caught the scent; it was thick inside. There was an impressive display of candles; perhaps that was the fragrance that had attracted him here? There was also a display of stones and crystals, like the one around the cat's neck. Maybe he was getting somewhere.

He was so engrossed in his search; he almost didn't hear the shop clerk. Her melodic voice made him pause. Once he made eye contact, he had the sinking feeling his life would never be the same. The sentence he muttered to himself was both a prayer and a curse.

"An Elf. Fuck me."

2.
NATASHA

There was something very therapeutic about folding black lace panties on a Monday morning. Natasha had just opened her shop, Roots, for the day, so it wasn't busy. She liked mornings, it gave her a breather before the bustle in New York City began. She loved owning a lingerie and crystal shop next to Central Park and had a constant flow of customers via the surrounding apartments and rentals that bordered it. But there were days she got lost in the doldrums. The boring and stable life she once dreamed of wasn't what she had envisioned for herself anymore. An eternity was a long time to live alone, especially for an Elf so far from home. Her mourning was over, she was ready to move on.

The bell on the door caused her to place an automatic smile on her face and take a breath to offer her greeting. But the man's focused stride caused her to bite it back. He was on a mission. She watched as he strode around the room, to one display then another, taking more of an inventory of things rather than shopping. His behavior disturbed her.

He sniffed the air. It was as if he were trying to pick up a scent. So, if not just a creeper sniffing lingerie, was he looking for something or someone? Trying not to get too worked up, she put it in her mind that perhaps he had just caught the fruity scent of the candles she'd just put out on display.

Another deep breath calmed the panic she had lived with since she had left home with her mortal lover. She missed the sense of stability she always had with him. Though he had long since passed, she still thought of him in times of stress. He had been her protector and friend. There had been a few who earned her trust as the years went on, but she had never been able to grant her heart as easily as access to her body.

"Can I help you?" Her voice had cracked, so she found her center and tried again. "Is there something I can help you find?" That was better but a little quieter, and yes, she had taken a step back.

After being in business so long, she had thought she'd seen it all, but nothing had prepared her for this. He was walking up to the shelves and pulling in a deep breath with his face practically on the fabric in her displays. Another step back.

"Are you looking for anything in particular? Those satin lacies just came in."

His behavior was beyond odd. He glanced her way with immediate dismissal as if he could see right through her then followed his nose. Goddess, help her. Was he another tracker? She thought those days were over.

She moved behind the sales counter mainly to give herself a barrier between his behavior and her comfort level, but also to have access to her phone which she had left by the register. He drew scents into his lungs, eyes closed with a slight smile curving his full lips, as if he had just caught the edge of something exquisite. She agreed her candles smelled amazing, but this man was having a a full on relationship with them. He lifted polished stones and crystals, turned them to catch the light, before placing them back into the display. Much as she enjoyed watching him admire her displays, she held back a simultaneous sigh of frustration. She had just finished organizing them. That area, by far, was the area she spent the most time in.

One more turn around her display and then he looked up. When they finally made eye contact, it felt as if her heart had stopped. She couldn't tell from this distance, but was there a bit of hazel in those dark eyes? It was like biting into her favorite chocolate and finding flecks of golden caramel inside. After a few seconds of reminding herself to breathe, he lowered his gaze and continued his shopping. He was less frantic now, as if realizing where he was and taking it all in. His answer to her earlier question, gravelly and masculine, hit her in the lady bits.

"No, thank you. Just looking."

Maid, mother, and crone…that voice. The thought occurred to her that there were plenty of the panties she had just been folding that would happily drop to the floor at his mere request. His voice was like velvet soothed over a silky thigh. She tried to place where she might've heard it before. Most likely in her dreams after reading one of the romance novels she liked so well. There was nothing she loved more than a story about a silver-tongued shifter, and his voice would sound amazing reading one of those.

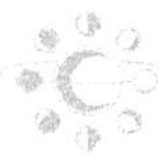

Perhaps if she got him talking? "Okay, well let me know if you find anything interesting."

Oh, dear goddess, did she just say that? The grin on his face as he caught her eye once more let her know they were on the same train of thought. His next comment and the way his eyes scanned over her curves confirmed it.

"You'll be the first to know." It wasn't necessarily what he said, but how it rolled off his tongue, as if the innuendo was an appetizer and he was preparing for the main course. He distracted her beyond reason, and she busied herself with straightening the tissue and bags behind her counter.

His pace was leisurely now, and he took his time looking at all the displays she had painstakingly rearranged. Somehow, watching him prowl around her showroom didn't bother her as much now. Especially considering, from her vantage point, she had a full view of his amazing ass. There was nothing she liked more on a man than a nice fitting pair of trousers. The time she took organizing her showroom when she opened had paid off. It was keeping this customer browsing a little longer.

When he found her friend's book display he turned her way with a questioning look as he pointed to the display.

"You have quite a mix of offerings."

"Those are from my friend's shop, Turn The Page. She's right up the street."

He picked up a book and made his way to the register, pulling out his wallet as he came closer. "I'll take this one."

She looked down at the title and remembered what she and her friend Alice had joked about. *"If a hot man buys this book, you need to get his number."*

She had argued at the time that if a hot man purchased a how-to book on how to satisfy a woman, he most likely had a woman in mind. She cleared her throat and reached for the paperback, taking note of his ringless hand without tan lines. After scanning the bar code, she looked up into his devilishly handsome face and felt a flush rise from the base of her neck. He totally caught where her line of vision had gone, had even spread apart the fingers of his hands on the counter to give her a good look. Goddess help her, even his hands were sexy.

"Research," he said with a dimpled smirk. He had to be messing with her. There was no way a man that looked and smelled like him needed a book like that. In fact, she would be shocked if he couldn't write one himself.

"That will be $26.49. And buy what you want, but it seems silly to me to buy a book for the content when the answer is right there on the cover." Her pale cheeks pinkened at the otherwise innocuous flirting.

He laughed and the sound of it was a balm to her soul. It was genuine and warm, like being wrapped up in her Sunday afternoon sherpa. At the same time, it made her acutely and desperately aware she was alone. She was tired of living in fear.

"I suppose you are right. My guess is if she comes first, the rest sort of settles into place. It will still be interesting to see what he says." He handed her two twenty-dollar bills, and as she made change as her mind conjured up the sound of his voice calling out her name as she "settled" on him and rode him like a stallion. The fact that she still thought his behavior was odd had no effect on her breasts which were now saying good morning. She really needed to get laid.

"$13.51 is your change." She stuffed the book in a logo-less bag and pushed it across the counter. He needed to go; these unexplainable emotions were getting hard for her to regulate. One minute she wanted to jump on him, the next she wanted to cry. Maybe that double-shot of expresso at breakfast hadn't been a good idea after all.

After one more slow intake of breath, he turned his head and looked her over one last time like he was taking a leisurely lick of a lollipop. He graced her with a dazzling smile. There was only one word for it. Magic.

"Thank you for your time, Miss."

As he walked past her to the door, she managed a squeak, like the timid mouse she was around men his size.

"Thanks for coming."

He paused with his hand on the door, the raised eyebrow completely did her in.

"It was my pleasure."

A chuckle before he opened the door and left her show room confirmed that he had the same warped sense of humor. Thanks for coming? Really? She should know better than to say something like that in a lingerie shop, especially to a man who was pleasure personified and just bought a book on how to please your woman. She walked to the thermostat and turned down the temp. It was much too warm already, and she had a long, hard day ahead of her.

What the…? Mind securely in the gutter. She rolled her eyes at herself and muttered a small prayer for strength. "Hecate, help me." She had a feeling it would take a lot more than the help of her patron goddess to get him out of her mind.

3
SAM

Sam was still smiling as he walked up Broadway back to his apartment. The petite store clerk wasn't his type, wasn't even the same species if he thought long and hard about it—not that any of that mattered. He was into her vibe and a relationship between shifters and elves wasn't unheard of. He had been right about the cat; she had been good luck. Once she stopped him, it didn't take much for him to be pulled in by his dick, which had gone hard six paces from the door.

He had never experienced such a powerful pull but had heard stories from others in his pack about finding their mates. The craze his brother went through was part of the reason Sam left in the first place. He had no desire to go through all of that and intended to never get married. He was married to his work and his life was here. The entire notion was a romanticized idea, but one that had him checking the store just in case. He knew the risks if she was nearby and he didn't follow through.

Now he was stuck. He hadn't been looking for his mate, frankly, that's why he moved to New York so many years ago. If anything, it was the exact opposite. He wanted nothing to do with that entire process nor did he ever want to claim his birthright and take on that responsibility. His brother was doing a fine job as Alpha after Sam had abdicated his right, so he was of the mindset to continue to let him do it. But what if she was something more than she seemed? What if she was the soulmate he wrote about in the books he created?

He shook her vision from his head and took a deep breath to center himself. Focus. He couldn't afford to have his head tripping down yet another distraction. The book wasn't going to write itself. Nor would his agent like it if he missed his deadline yet again. The edits were taking forever this time, but his hero and heroine were missing something which was, in part, what prompted the walk. Well that and the panties. The fresh air sometimes helped to clear the cobwebs, but all it did this time was send him straight into a situation that would most likely stay with him the rest of the week.

He thought back over the last several moon cycles, to the blackouts which had gotten progressively worse since he rented his new apartment a year ago. They were more manageable when he lived in Jersey, but now that he lived in the city, they had strengthened each and every month since. He used to remember what he had done, now it was all a blur. Tying himself to his bed each moon cycle was the only way he could ensure he didn't hurt anyone or expose himself now that he was in the public eye. Too bad it was getting increasingly hard to control himself. But in the store, around her, it was like being in a hot spring. Calming warmth and beauty surrounded him, and just being near her brought him a peace he had never known. The stuff of dreams. His detour into the shop was unexpected, as was finding his mate, and now he needed to figure out what to do about it.

Foregoing the cold shower, he sat at his desk and opened his laptop. He had never attempted writing with a raging hard-on, but who was to say it wouldn't work. He went back to the beginning and read through the chapter, stopping along the way and reworking the character he had created. Her goal, motivation, and conflict or GMC was strong, but if he wasn't feeling it for her, why would his reader? What was it that he liked about her, or about women in general? It was never about beauty for him necessarily, more about the quiet strength they exuded. Like they had all the answers and if you were lucky, they would let you in on the secrets of the Universe. Gods help you if you ever found yourself on their bad side though, because being on the outside of their favor was something to be feared. He found that kind of strength undeniably hot.

As he read through his heroine's characteristics and the way she saw herself, visions of the timid brunette came to his mind. His heroine was typical of what he had been attracted to in the past, athletic build, blonde, long hair, and eyes the color of the clear sky. But from the bulge in his pants, this project needed something different. Apparently, so did he. Perhaps the blondes had been safe. His psyche knew deep down they wouldn't be soulmate material.

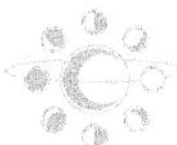

Before he knew it, the store clerk was being described in the pages, and his pulse started to match his libido. Shoulder length brown hair, honey-brown eyes like a doe, and a sweet, soft body that could be pulled into him like a feather pillow. He imagined lying next to her ass, curved against his ever-thickening penis, and he realized his mistake. On top of everything else, he was also editing the wrong scene.

Grabbing his pen and a half used legal pad he kept near his laptop at all times, he jotted a note to himself. She's a brunette — remember the Roots worker. He was onto something. He jotted one more thing as an afterthought. Sage and jasmine, her signature scent?

He pulled the black lace panties from his pocket, taking in the faded scent that had drawn him into the store in the first place. He ran his finger over the tiny gold tree of life sewn on the hip, the exact logo which he recognized from the front of the store. There was no denying the lacies which were draped over him this morning had come from there, they were identical to the pair he was holding. He was crazy to have taken them.

He could see it now, the headlines splashed all over the Times about the up-and-coming romance author getting arrested for his fetish and stalkerish behavior. His agent would drop him like a bad habit. But the mystery of the scent and how it was affecting him compelled him to do it. He looked down on the stolen panties, wondering if it would really be shoplifting if the panties were returned, then got up and went to the kitchen to get the bag to seal them inside with the other pair.

The scent hadn't come from the lingerie or the candles, it had been coming from her. He could still smell it, as if it had seeped into his pores. He smelled his hands, and sure enough, it was there like a calling card. The scent was connected to his memory, imprinted in his psyche like a tattoo. She had one, he'd noticed, the tree of life on the inside of her wrist slightly hidden by the gauzy red shrug that covered her shoulders. He liked her in red and wondered how she would look gazing back at him with those soulful brown eyes, after he made love to her on top of his favorite red chenille throw, or if she would be game to make love on a bed of soft moss in the forest. He wondered what she would look like in nothing else but the mysterious black panties that had found his way into his life. He wasn't sure, but he had a scene to write and found himself all sorts of inspired.

Happy he had found his Muse, he went back to editing, starting with the changes to the sex scene that had come to his mind fully formed. As he started to rework the scene, he realized the hero was starting to look a lot like him.

4
NATASHA

Tasha loved New York, with its ability to swallow people whole and hide them in its bowels. The move there 10 years ago was to do just that. Hide. She had seen a lot of crazy things in New York since her decision to grow roots, but she had never had anything happen to her remotely close to what she walked into when she opened her shop that day.

It wasn't uncommon for members of the homeless community to take refuge in her doorway at night. While she would often leave food, toiletries, or even clothing, she had never received a thank you quite like the one she found when she arrived Thursday. Two pairs of the black lace panties she had been folding earlier in the week were in a plastic bag taped to her door. There was no denying they were from her store, as identified by her Roots logo and the fact that the tags were still on them, but where they came from was a complete mystery.

It hadn't been so busy that she missed one of her regulars coming in and taking them. Besides, she knew they wouldn't do that, they watched out for her. Her memory snapped to the smoking hot man who came in Monday, perhaps he had taken them? Weird, but stranger things happened. The panties were neatly folded, didn't seem otherwise worse for wear, but she wasn't taking any chances. They went promptly into her garbage behind the counter, prior to washing her hands and getting on with her day.

After a busy afternoon, she decided to treat herself. She closed the shop then wandered down the block to her friend's store, Turn The Page. As always, Alice greeted her with a big hug before heading back to her seat and picking up the book she had been reading.

"I haven't seen you all week. Have you been busy?" Tasha glanced at the book's cover, curious as to what she was reading. It was a 4 star, something she had just finished.

"Yeah, strangely it has been busy. Makes me wonder if there's some sort of a convention going on."

"When isn't there one," Alice laughed.

"True. Just wondering if you have had anyone strange come in lately?"

"Like stranger than the strange I typically have come in?" She laughed with Tasha. "Why, you have someone strange? I mean, I find that really hard to believe with you owning a lingerie store and all."

"Yeah it is a mystery how we seem to attract them. I just had this guy come in on Monday and at first he was a little weird. I almost called you."

"Weird how?" Alice sat up in her seat and handed Tasha a diet soda before opening the lid to hers and taking a drink. That was Tasha's invitation to have a seat behind the counter.

"He started out sniffing candles like a dog, then pawed through my crystals. After a few minutes he beaded in on your book display and ended up buying one, said it was for research. So, I was curious if he had come in here to buy anything else."

"Which book? Please tell me it wasn't the one we…"

Tasha almost spit out her drink, her friend was scary sometimes with her intuition. "It was," she laughed.

"And…"

"And he was hotter than Hades."

"And… did you get his number?"

"No, I didn't get his number, I'm sure he was going home to try his research out on his girlfriend. A very lucky, lucky, girlfriend."

"That good huh?"

Tasha nodded. "I won't be able to dream of another man as long as I live. Every man I read will have his face from now on."

"Considering we read more Romance than the average person, I would say that he comes highly recommended. I'm bummed he didn't come in here. I would have loved to check out your walking, talking, Adonis."

"Adonis was a little too classically beautiful for me. I like them a little grittier. Speaking of which, do you have anything new by A.M. Wolfe? Now he writes some yummy heroes."

"Totally agree, but his book isn't out for another few months. I do have some new romantasies you might like though."

Tasha shook her head. "Elves aren't really my thing. The heroes are sort of…" she scrunched her nose as a way of explaining.

"Stinky?"

"Sometimes," Tasha laughed. "Mostly wimpy little tools that use their wealth and prestige as a way to get what they want."

Alice scrunched her face. "Ummm, I will beg to differ. You didn't see Legolas doing any of that."

"Legolas was a fictional character," Tasha laughed. She got up and pointed toward the back of the store. She knew how Alice felt about the Fae, but what she didn't know was that Tasha had first-hand knowledge of what the little weasels were really like. That was a conversation for another day. It still wasn't safe to share. "I'll just browse around. I'm sure I'll be able to find something."

"Probably not something you haven't already read." Alice laughed. "This one is good, thanks for the recommendation."

"No problem. I thought you would like it. By the way, do you want to get a drink with me after you close? I was thinking about stopping at the Tea Room on my way home."

"Too rich for my blood. Besides, I've got a date tonight with Tommy. You should join us, nobody should drink alone."

"Maybe next time. Tell him I said hi. And I'm never alone when I've got a good book."

"That is very true and I will. By the way, I don't know how you read those steamy scenes out in public though and not show a reaction. I end up getting so hot and bothered, I'm practically jumping on Tommy, even if I'm pissed at him. I can hardly stand to help customers when they walk in on me here at the store."

Tasha laughed and shrugged. "Hiding emotions is a secret power I have, I guess."

"You'll have to let me in on that secret sometime," Alice said. "It would help me get a lot more books read. By the way, we're still on for Sunday afternoon, right?"

"Absolutely! Looking forward to it!"

"Sweet, I'll bring the wine. I should be to your place around 3 o'clock."

"I'll be ready, closing by 1 o'clock that day. I'll whip something up to eat since I will be home a few hours before you get there."

Sounds perfect. Love everything you have ever made me. Have fun browsing, the new stuff is on the table there. You know your way around."

"I certainly do! My home away from home."

After purchasing a fantastic-looking paranormal romance debut, Tasha made her way around the corner to one of her favorite places in the world. Alice was right, The Russian Tea Room was a bit high end, but she absolutely loved the atmosphere. The charismatic man who came into her shop was still on her mind for more reasons than one. After not sensing a tracker in some time, she had let her guard down, leaning into a false sense of comfort in the hordes of people who lived here. Sexy or no, his visit had put her on edge.

No longer feeling invisible, she scanned the crowds during her walk. The habit had saved her life more than once, and the threat was still out there. She needed to be more aware of her surroundings. She thought back on her walk to the bookstore, the prickling on the back of her neck. Recalling the crowds in her mind, had there been someone? The blonde man across the street, facing her motionless in the crowd? Had he been watching her or merely standing on the curb to catch a cab? Was she being neurotic?

Her pace was brisk, and her eye contact cursory. No one was paying her any mind. She looked over the shoulders of the people coming toward her, men and women alike, all who could be sent by those who sought her out. The people on the street had better things to do than to pay any attention to an elf on the run. Making it to the restaurant in record time, she slipped under the canopy and walked inside the safe space. The protection spells woven into the land had seeped into the building with each renovation it had lived through since the late 1800s. She gave thanks to those who came before her each time she drank here.

Even though her thoughts now had her on edge, she decided it wasn't going to hurt to stay for one drink and read a few chapters of her book. Besides, she hadn't seen her friend, Jasmine, the barkeep there, in some time. Even when it was busy, they were able to catch up on the neighborhood gossip over a Cosmonaut or two. With book in hand, she entered the gilded cherry-red and hunter-green room and gave a wink to the smiling image of Felix the Cat. She veered left, and with a nod and wave to Jasmine, she slid into the seat on the end of the bar closest to the wall. Within minutes she was sipping her favorite drink. Jasmine apologized for not being able to chat, a large party had come in for an early dinner, and she was hopping. Tasha waved her off. She completely understood since the last time Jasmine came in her store, she had a line at the register.

The drink went down smoothly, and the chapters caused the ambient conversation to fade into the background. Finally, her calm state had returned. She loved getting lost in a story, the escape it provided during times of stress was priceless. Books were the only thing that had kept her sane during the worst times of her life. Some might think it odd, but they were some of her closest friends. Some of her first editions had been through a lot with her.

This was a new-to-her author and so far, it was holding her interest.

The shifters were hot marshmallow alphas that let the women pave the way and supported them no matter what crazy idea came into their head. The sex was uninhibited and loving, carefree in its spontaneity. And no matter if the heroes had all the answers, they allowed the heroines to come to it in their own time, in their own way. That was probably the vibe in Alpha stories she was most fond of…unquestioning loyalty and patience. Add a bit of forced proximity and sprinkle in a secret past, and you had a five star in her opinion.

After two drinks and a couple of waters, she cashed out then went downstairs to use the restroom. As she always did when she visited the restaurant, she walked along the displays of Russian nesting dolls, admiring the detail of some of the older pieces. The voice that startled her from her musings simultaneously soothed and jangled her nerves.

"I always thought the wolf was misunderstood."

A deep breath centered her. The realization that he wouldn't be able to enter a space she was afforded protection had her biting her lip to hold back a laugh. As she recognized the man from her shop, she pondered again at where she might have heard his voice. Perhaps he was an audio book narrator?

She knew before she glanced over her shoulder that he was about a foot behind her. The pulse of his energy against hers was hard to ignore. Her eyes were level with his chest, so she craned her neck back to see his face. He was noticeably taller now that she was in her comfortable flat shoes. He was pointing at the Fairy Tale nesting doll she had been admiring.

"Well, considering he ate Red's Grandmother then disguised himself as her, I can see how that happened." The grin on his face gave her courage to let down her guard. He was truly fun to banter with. She felt comfortable enough on a second meeting, knowing he wasn't there to harm her, to be more herself.

"Ah, but was that what really happened?" He bent down so his head was level with hers, which allowed him to quiet their conversation, making it seem much more intimate than being in a hallway lined with curio cabinets just a few steps away from the restrooms.

No matter the space, he had her attention. She faced him and registered amusement in his dark eyes, like he was about to share a delicious secret. Their rich mocha depths were flecked with golden caramel, she had been right, and his gaze was melting over her like the chocolate she craved every night.

His musk came through the earthy cologne he wore, and it made her wonder why he even bothered wearing it. He smelled delicious and she caught herself closing her eyes to draw the scent into her lungs. If only she could make him into a candle scent, she would burn him day and night. He did something to her, calmed her in a way she hadn't felt in decades… centuries even. Being close to him messed with her sensibilities.

He continued as if he didn't notice her odd behavior around him, even though she fully well knew from his knowing grin, he did. "According to the stories, that is precisely what happened. With various versions having him eat other people as well."

"I agree with the eating bit. Which version did you read?" It was the smirk that got her attention and he knew it.

"Brothers Grimm. But I take it you already knew that."

"I did," he chuckled. "I prefer the original. The Charles Perrault version. When Red slips off her clothes and gets into bed with the wolf, the word 'eat' takes on a whole new meaning." He waited until her face had flushed before finishing his thought. "Wouldn't you agree?"

Her voice cracked. "I haven't read that version. Perhaps I should do some research."

He took a step toward her, unbelievably they were close enough she could feel his heat, but far enough apart to be appropriate in a public space. His warm minty breath tickled the side of her neck as he leaned to speak in hushed tones. "I'd be happy to help research anything you find of interest."

Inhale, Tasha. Since when had she forgotten how to breathe? So much for not showing emotions. "Thank you…" The question in her tone had him taking a step back and standing straight before responding.

"Sam. Sam Randall."

He paused, and then she offered hers. "Natasha Vera. My friends call me Tasha." He held out his hand for hers, and when she offered it, he grasped her fingers and raised her hand up. In another world, and perhaps with the continued sensibilities relating to hygiene, the warmth of a man's lips on the ridge of her knuckles would be unwelcome. But in her world, with this man, it was fate. She pulled back her hand, already missing the feel of his lips.

"Nice to meet you, Sam. Now tell me, how do you know so much about fairy tales?"

"How much time do you have?"

"I closed my store, so I have all night."

Her response prompted a smile. It lit the small hallway they were standing in. "I'm starved. Have you eaten?" She couldn't help but laugh considering their recent conversation. A quick shake of her head was all he needed before pulling her up the stairs. "Perfect. I know just the spot."

5
NATASHA

To her surprise and utter delight, he walked her right out the door of the restaurant and across the street to the hot dog cart at the entrance to Central Park. After getting the vendor's attention, he glanced over to her with a question in his brow.

"Everything?"

"Of course," she laughed. "What respectable New Yorker wouldn't get it loaded?"

Sam turned back to the vendor and held his fingers up in a "v." "Two please. Also, two chips and…" He looked to Tasha for a response.

"Diet."

"One diet, one regular."

The vendor was already on it, and the exchange was over in a matter of minutes. They carried their meal to the nearest bench, and Tasha nudged her head. "You can go up further. I like to be away from the hum of the cars."

Sam smiled at that and kept walking until he reached a secluded bench far from the street.

"This is perfect." She handed him her food then pulled her large square shawl from her bag and draped it in the center of the seat before sitting on one side of it. After placing her bag on the end of the bench, she pointed to the space next to her. "Sit here. They wash up easily. It will keep you from getting your pants dirty." She took the food he passed back to her and had already taken a big bite of her hot dog before he settled completely next to her.

Some of the relish mix slid from his hot dog as he took a bite, landing squarely on the top of his thigh. "Too late," he joked.

She was already reaching into her bag for the hand wipes she kept on hand. "Try one of these, it may keep them from staining."

"Thanks." As he wiped, she attempted to concentrate more on her dinner than the area he was cleaning. She didn't want to seem as if she was gawking, but this man was built. She held up a baggie next. "You can put it in here."

"Is there anything you don't have in that bag?"

"I like being prepared for anything," she answered. "It's what I love about New York, there are always last-minute opportunities. Take to-night, for instance."

"Good point." He put the used wipe in the bag and set it next to him, juggling the half-eaten hot dog in the other. It was gone in a few bites. When he looked up, she was holding out another wipe which he used for his hands. "You're a regular Mary Poppins."

She had just finished and was leaning back enjoying her drink. "Well, you will be getting a spoonful of sugar drinking that. How can you stand regular? It's so sweet."

He grinned. "I like sweet stuff. I'm here with you, aren't I?"

"Good point," she threw back at him with a grin. She liked this easy-going side of him. It was much different from the first impression she had. Everyone was allowed to have a bad day, perhaps his was earlier in the week. "So, what is it you do, other than take strange women out for a gourmet meal in the middle of Central Park?"

"I'm a writer."

Her pulse quickened. She didn't know many authors and had so many questions. "I love books. What sort of stuff do you write?"

"A bit of Fantasy, a little Romance, and right now, I'm working on a Fairy Tale retelling."

"Let me guess."

He shook his head laughing. "Red was the last one. My current book is based on a tale which is a little less known. The Prince and the Gray Wolf."

"I know that one. With a firebird, right?" He nodded, and her head connected the dots. It couldn't possibly be. "So like A.M. Wolfe?"

His smile lit his eyes. "You've read me?"

"Like a book, apparently," she gushed. "I love your work. Your references to the fairy tale back at the restaurant make so much sense now." On remembering the contents of his last book, she flushed. Some of the scenes between the wolf and Red were five out of five on her spice scale. Her next question had her clearing her throat. "So where do you get your ideas?" She was intrigued by how he would respond.

He turned in his seat to face her then leaned his head on his hand, elbow securely on the back of the bench. Somehow, he didn't look as casual as he should have. He looked very much like he would like to show her precisely where he got his ideas. Strangely, she would be all for it.

"I live in New York," he answered simply. "There is no shortage of ideas in a city like this. How about you? What is your story?"

That he changed the subject didn't go unnoticed. She gave the annotated PG version of her story. There was no way she would ever trust anyone again with the full truth. She was finally feeling settled. "I moved here about 10 years ago on a whim. I met Charlotte, the owner of Roots, shortly after I moved into town, and she offered me a job. I've been there ever since."

"It's a nice shop. You must like it there."

"I do, the boss is great." The online store had an image of a beautiful blonde who Tasha had hired as a model. Keeping her name and face off the internet had been something she had learned to do the hard way. Being the employee of a fictional boss was the easiest way for her to keep a low profile.

"And what about the cat? Does she belong to you or the owner?"

"Cat?" She was curious how he would have gotten that idea.

He nodded. "Black, with a green gem on her collar. Sassy."

"Not mine," she shrugged. "But there are some strays that I put food out for. I'm guessing she was looking for her next meal."

"Yeah, she acted like it. Pretty much pounced on me outside your shop. Practically chased me through the door."

"I'm kind of glad she did." Natasha's cheeks warmed at her confession.

Her pulse fluttered with his.

"Me too."

He shifted his arm closer, his hand gently rubbing the top of her shoulder. She leaned into it, allowing the pressure of his touch to strengthen. The rhythmic circles of his thumb were doing strange things to her senses. It had been far too long since she had known a man's touch. She ached to know it once more. The next admission slipped out and surprised her.

"I hardly know you." Her hand lightly touching his chest as she leaned toward him and made her comment was as close to consent as she could utter without embarrassing herself. She wasn't sure if the attraction she was feeling was reciprocal. When she looked into his eyes, there was no denying the fire.

"You've read me. You probably know me better than anyone. I'm found in the words I write."

She slid even closer, mesmerized by his aura and heat. Her pulse quickened as her mind went to her favorite scene in his latest book, and she swallowed the croak in her throat that formed there. Images of Red riding her wolf in nothing but the cloak he had given her replayed in her mind. The passion that had come to her off the page was magical, and anyone who could write relationship fiction like that was someone worth knowing.

Her next comment came out in a whisper. "I've been alone a long time." He had no idea how long. Did she really want to put her trust in someone again? If so, did she really want to relive the pain of losing another person she gave a piece of her heart to? The solitude was weakening her resistance, she was tired of being alone. And this man was interesting, and compelling, and hot as fuck.

He cupped her cheek and traced the outline of her lips with his thumb. The conversation turned from playful banter to quiet intimacy in seconds.

"There has been no one for me either. I live alone and have been content to do so, but I'll be honest, I really want to…"

Yes! There was no mistaking his meaning, and she was straddling his lap and kissing him before he could finish. The dress she was wearing tented over the parts of them that were becoming acquainted, and the friction of fabric against skin was something she was sure she would pay for later. She didn't care. It felt good to be safe in a man's arms again. Good to be rubbing up against the proof of the attraction he felt for her.

"I love the way you smell. Your taste." He was kissing the sweet spot on her neck now, and she leaned her head over to give him full access. "You have been all I've thought about this week." The stubble on his cheeks felt so good, as did the warmth of his tongue tasting her between tiny nibbles along her collarbone. "Gods, Tasha, you are perfection."

She smiled at the admission then placed her hands on his cheeks to pull him in for another kiss. His hands slid to her ass and pulled her into his groin. She hadn't thought it could get any bigger, but she had been wrong. Lost in the feeling, she tipped her head back giving him full access to her breasts which easily slipped from the top of the corset style top on her dress. He was lapping, and she looked side to side before reaching for her bag and making her next move.

It was late, the police had just gone by, and by her calculation, they had less than 20 minutes to pull it off. If no one else came, that was. She raised up on her knees and slid her hand down under her dress and between her legs to the bulge she had been happily riding for the past few minutes. Two sighs of relief sounded at the pull of his zipper, and when she looked up, he said six words that the ex she ran away from would have never uttered.

"We don't have to do this."

Six words that had her pulling his dick from his pants and slipping on a condom. "Oh, yes we do. You have no idea."

"Mary Poppins." The smile on his face was the frosting on the cupcake. She placed herself over him and pulled small gasps from him as she teased her way down. He felt so good, filling her completely. She had missed the feel of a man inside her as she relished the breeze on her bare skin. The swaying of nearby branches in the moonlight added to the magick of the moment, while the rustling of the leaves helped to cover their contented moans.

"You work at a lingerie store but don't wear panties?" His question caught her off guard and she snorted.

He licked what he could reach as they passed by his lips. Neck, breasts, nipples, were all fair game until she was fully seated. Once she was, her head was fully in the crook of his neck, and he rose up to meet her. She was still laughing.

"I took them off earlier, they were riding up." At her admission he started to move faster.

"I fucking love when that happens."

His chuckle had her laughing once more. When was the last time she felt this free, this alive? He bucked, and she rode, holding tight to his shoulders and relishing the feel of his hand grasping her ass. She would have bruises for sure, but these she wouldn't mind. His other hand slipped between her legs and he pushed on her core. The friction and pressure of his finger was just what she needed.

"Oh, Mother Goddess. Almost there, Sam. This won't be quiet."

"I'm counting on it. Muffle it with a kiss, love."

And she did. Wild and ravenous, she crashed against him like the ocean against the shore. Kissed him until she found her release and moaned into his waiting mouth as he found his own. There was no sense of time or place, no sense of urgency or obligation. Just two souls connecting in a world of their making. Safety. She was surrounded by it and it filled the gaps in her soul like nothing else ever had. Who was this man that Fate had sent her way?

He lessened the pressure of his finger but kept rubbing to draw every tremor of pleasure, causing her to shudder at the slightest move. She couldn't hold back the giggle; her heart was filled with complete joy, and the endorphins were at work. Complete relaxation and con-nection. Her head rested back down on his shoulder as he slipped his hand away and straightened her dress. He held her with one arm tight to him, the other remained at his side. Her heart had just slowed to a normal rhythm when she heard the footsteps.

"Everything okay here?" The voice startled her, but the pressure of his arm kept her from moving.

"Yes, officer," Sam answered. "She's just had a bit much to drink. Let-ting her sleep some of it off before we go home and relieve the sitter."

"Mam?"

"I'm good occifer." Tasha giggled and cuddled into Sam for effect. "Just enjoying quiet time without the babies."

"Know how the date night thing goes. Seems the wife and I get to do that less and less these days. Enjoy your evening."

"We will. You too." They said in unison.

As the sound of the footsteps receded, she raised her head and looked at him with chagrin. "I'm feeling better, honey. Should we go home and pay the sitter?"

"It was all I could come up with in a pinch, considering that I'm still inside you and needed to get rid of him quickly."

"I can feel why. But you can't be comfortable."

"I would argue that I have the best seat in the house. But yes, we probably shouldn't risk staying for his next check. You wouldn't happen to have an extra pair of trousers in that bag, would you?"

She reached over and pulled out her wipes along with a fleece jacket. "Nope, but this should help get you presentable enough to get home to the kids."

6
SAM

Distracted. Edgy. Agitated. He didn't need a thesaurus to further describe what he was feeling, nor did he need to research the root cause. He pictured her face every time he closed his eyes.

Eyes. Hers were soulful… warm… laughing.

Lips. Inviting… luscious… heart-shaped.

Expressions. Delighted… intrigued… desire-filled.

Body….Fuck.

He had it bad.

Not that he needed to, but he looked at the calendar and counted the days. He had been right, twelve more and he would be out of his fucking mind.

Time to buy stronger restraints.

What in Hades was he going to do about her?

7
NATASHA

Tasha had just put the finishing touches on the Caprese salad and put the spinach-artichoke dip in the oven when the doorbell rang. "Be right there," she called out to the door. She checked the peephole then opened the door for Alice.

"I'm still not sure how on a manager's salary you afford this place," she said as she put the wine she brought down on the counter. "I can barely afford a place big enough to hold a queen mattress and a toilet, and you have an industrial studio loft that looks like a conservatory."

"I told you before, I have a trust fund," Tasha laughed uncomfortably. She hated having to lie, but over 500 years of accumulated wealth was impossible to explain.

"Must be nice," Alice winked.

"If you knew my father you wouldn't think so. In fact, you would probably say I deserved a raise." Tasha busied herself with setting up their evening activity and hoped the flippant comment would be ignored.

"Yeah, picked up on that over the years. We should compare and contrast one day soon. But tonight, I'm focusing on removing a crappy boyfriend from my life." She was already pulling two wineglasses from Tasha's shelves over the kitchen sink. "You want me to open the red or white?"

"I'm taking it the date didn't go well the other night. White is perfect."

Alice shook her head as she worked on the cork. "It hasn't been going great for a while. I was just in denial."

Tasha was relieved to move on from the earlier line of questioning. "I'm always up for taking care of crappy boyfriends. You sure you want to go there with Tommy?"

"Pretty sure." Alice hung her purse on one of the bar chairs lining the counter Tasha used as a table, then picked up the glasses and walked to where her friend sat in the living room. Tasha took the wine she was offered, took a sip, then got back to organizing the essential oils in alphabetical order. "I'm sure I have all the ingredients you will need for a communication spell. I also have the cauldron you have been using on the end table if you have something to burn."

Alice nodded and relaxed into one of the papasan chairs Tasha had across from the couch. "Thanks. I'm working on a banishment spell this time. I'm through with communicating. Tommy isn't getting it."

"Isn't banishment a bit harsh?" Tasha questioned.

"Not for someone who has been cheating on me."

That got Tasha's attention. She looked incredulously at Alice shaking her head in confusion. "Who in their right mind would mess around on you? He is a dumb ass."

Alice smiled sadly, calming the tears that were forming with a sip of her wine. "Thanks Tash, I appreciate you so much."

"Just stating a fact," Tasha shrugged. "Cheers." They clinked their glasses, and then Tasha rummaged through her selection of oils and handed Alice a few. "Here are rosemary, lavender, and wormwood."

"Always the perfect start," Alice laughed. "Can you hand me the clove oil?"

"Perfect choice to represent you and create a barrier."

"That is what I thought," Alice nodded. "Did you bring out your box of dried herbs also? I think I want to pull this all together and try some candle magick with it. It seems as though I should add some fire to this spell."

"He's a goner," Tasha laughed. "Wish I could say it was nice knowing him, but honestly, I never really vibed with him. I mean, how you could date a non-reader in the first place is beyond me."

"That was truly the first of many red flags," Alice agreed. "I don't know what I was thinking, truly."

"You didn't want to be alone. I get it."

"Well, you're single and thriving. It's not like we couldn't have sex with any number of attractive men we meet in our day-to-day interactions." After the few seconds of silence, Alice looked up and shot a knowing look at Tasha. "You met someone."

"Maybe," Tasha answered quietly. She was still reeling about that night and stood to pace the floor with her glass.

"You more than met someone. You had sex! Mother goddess, Tash, this is huge!"

"I'm not sure how I feel about it yet."

"Well, considering I've known you a decade and have never seen you with anyone, this is monumental! This spell can wait, I want to hear all about it." Alice ran to the kitchen to get the open bottle of wine and returned to the couch. Topping off their glasses, she plopped herself down and shot Tasha a grin. "Okay, spill."

"I'm not sure how much there is to spill," Tasha said still pacing. "I mean, we just met… got together… oh, stars above!"

"When you pull out 'stars above' I know you are frustrated," Alice mused. "Okay start from the beginning, when did you meet?"

"Remember when I told you about the guy who came in on Monday?"

Alice's eyes widened. "Not the guy who bought the how-to book on how to give a woman an orga…"

"One and the same."

"And?"

Tasha shook her head and laughed. "And he didn't need the blasted book, could have written it as a matter of fact. As it turns out, it was A.M. Wolfe. His name is Sam."

Alice shot up from the couch. "Are you serious right now?" She hesitated as Tasha nodded then paced some more. "You had sex with A.M. Wolfe? The A.M. Wolfe?"

Tasha nodded and flopped down in the papasan across from Alice. "Apparently."

In a daze, Alice sat on the couch and picked up her wineglass. "Well cheers to that. So, what does he look like? I always found it interesting that he didn't have an Author Bio picture in his books."

"He's insanely handsome, built like a marble statue, and has a dry wit and charisma that stops my breath. He is like a fragrant breeze in a heather-filled meadow, a soothing dip in a sparkling river, the warmth of the sun on your outstretched arms."

"When you pull out the lyrical language, I know you are invested. Why do I sense that there is a 'but' in your comment?"

"Because there is," Tasha shrugged. "I haven't heard from him since. It's so strange too because I feel as though we connected beyond the sex. He was all the things I never thought I would find in a partner again. Warm, thoughtful, considerate, interesting. I mean, I haven't dated in a while, but it seems to me that if he were truly interested in me, I would have heard from him by now."

"He could be super busy," Alice offered. "Maybe on a deadline or something. I would give it a few days. Maybe we could do a spell for you as well?"

"I think I will let Fate play this one out. Dabbling in the outcome isn't my thing. I'm more of a meditate and it will come to me kind of gal. You know that. In the meantime, we will work on getting you on track for better options. Tommy doesn't deserve you, and we should just wish him well and send him on his way and I know just the spell to start with."

Tasha went to her bookshelf and pulled down her leatherbound grimoire. After unlatching the clasp, she flipped the ancient pages until she came to the spell she had been given by a witch she had met centuries before in Salem. It had been how she had gathered most of the information in this book, since she was not a sorceress, per se. The innate skills she was born with couldn't easily be used in this world, at least not without bringing attention to herself and her knowledge of potions and spells was limited.

"I can't get over how old that book looks. I really need you to help me make one. How do you get the pages to look so archaic? They are practically creaking."

"I've had this for years," Tasha muttered. "We can get you a journal filled with art stock as a base, like I did."

"I love how you have examples taped inside. Leaves and such. I may have to copy some of your recipes to start."

"Absolutely," Tasha said. "The best way to practice magick, is to share your knowledge with others. I'm happy to pass on what I know."

She stopped flipping when reaching the spell she felt would be best for Alice's soon-to-be ex. "You sure about the banishment?" It was the same one she had been using for centuries, one she was sure needed to be refreshed again. It had been a while.

Alice nodded. "Yup. Don't want him anywhere near me in the future. If it means he will need to pack up and move, so mote it be."

"Alright, let's get to it."

8

SAM

Sam was in trouble. He stared at the number on his phone and hesitated to push it, just as he had done several times a day for the past week. They had exchanged numbers after stopping at her store for another round. Rounds. The padded benches in the dressing rooms were much more comfortable than the park bench, and while it was her idea, he still felt bad that they hadn't made love in a bed. Even through its mid-cycle, the moon was stronger than he had realized. Now creeping into waxing gibbous, he continued to worry about the full moon and how it would impact them both. Who knew if the restraints he bought would even hold.

Considering the amount of editing he had left, perhaps having sex with her on the park bench had been a mistake. Maybe not so much that, as the second time in the pink and white changing room of her store, when he kneeled before her and feasted between her satin legs like she was a buffet. She smelled so sweet. He was pretty sure it was the third time, when he took her from behind against the panty display, that he had truly lost his mind…and his heart. It was also his cue to call it a night, with fangs poking through his gumline and tempting him to mark her as his. Thankfully, they had been hidden from her view as he rammed into her, bent over the black lace panties that brought her into his life. He bit back the howl until his walk home, then let it loose in the alleyway near his apartment. The sex in her store had been her idea, but he hadn't fought it. Now he wanted much more, but she hadn't called. Neither had he.

There was no denying the chemistry they had, but was that all it was for him? Was it some weird mate thing that messed with his brain? He never fully understood the mating pull, but if it was an endless yearning to be by her side, to know what she thought, to understand what moved her, then he had it bad. It was as if no one else on the planet mattered, and it scared the ever-living fuck out of him.

He couldn't even do proper research on it since anything written about Weres in this world was completely fictional, except some of the stuff he wrote, of course, which he would never market as "own voices." The only way he would know for sure was to go home and ask his brother, but that wasn't something he was willing to do. Yet.

And what about for her? He was all for an independent woman making the moves, so why hadn't she? He thought they had both had an amazing time, but as each day went by without contact, he was less sure about it all. As much as he had researched the human condition and the way they navigated relationships, it sure didn't prepare him for one. He was especially ill-equipped to handle one with an Elf. What the hell did he know about them, other than his father absolutely hated them? Thankfully, he didn't need to worry about his opinion anymore. And why the hell was she in New York surrounded by concrete and people? Didn't they like nature and solitude?

The only thing he knew for sure was that if he didn't see her again, there was no way he'd be finishing his book. She was imprinted on every single page, breathing between the lines of his prose and living in every corner of his mind. He didn't have the heart to see it through until things were resolved with them. But why would she want to be in his life, not knowing if the relationship was founded only on pheromones? That it all was based on a feeling he had no control over, not the connection of two hearts and minds? Impulse worked fine for a wolf on the hunt; it kept him fed. But for a relationship, the only thing it did was create friction and dismissal out of a warped sense of loyalty. At least, that was what he had seen with his parents and grandparents. They hated one another, but they always did what was best for the pack. That wasn't the life he chose, and he wouldn't force Tasha to make it hers, either. Loyalty had to be a choice for them both.

All he knew is that his editor was chomping at the bit to get his final edits, and he needed to do something. He wasn't a fan of phone conversations, and texts seemed too impersonal. What was compelling him to get ready to leave his apartment was the thought that if he had these compulsions and was as uncomfortable as he was at this moment, he needed to check on her. She needed to know he was thinking of her, and that she wasn't alone. She didn't need to agree to be in his life, although he hoped now that could be an option, but he wanted to make sure she was okay. That he had been considering rearranging his bachelorhood and making space in his life for her in his mind, was something that still amazed him. In his wildest dreams, he never thought this would happen to him.

He put on a pressed dress shirt, his favorite shade of green, and picked up his wallet before heading out the door. He wondered what kind of flowers were her favorite and if the shop around the corner had time to make him something nice. Checking his watch, he decided he had enough time to get there before it closed for the night.

The selection at the shop had been much too formal, and it took him piecing things together from the buckets in the cooler to come up with exactly what he wanted. The florist bundled it in what he called a hand tied, finishing the piece with a few threads of raffia, which he learned about as they chatted. In his mind, it looked like twine but without the braiding, and it got him thinking it would be fun to write a series highlighting the floral industry. He had seen some cool stuff in the arrangements that he wondered about, some of which seemed to defy gravity and held the form into place by wires and twigs. He was sure he would regret falling down another rabbit hole of research, but he shrugged it off. Learning about things that interested him was the best part of being a writer.

He was still a few blocks away, when the smell of her fear overtook the fragrance of the bouquet he was carrying. It was dropped to the sidewalk as his feet started to move. He ran as if his life depended on it.

His hand was on the door as his eyes adjusted to the scene inside. He pulled it open, the old wooden frame banging against the inset doorway with a thunk. Even with the bell clanging to the floor and his heavy footsteps treading through the showroom, the man who had his back to him didn't move. Tasha's head was lowered to the side as the man caressed her cheek. Sam slowed his steps then turned down a nearby aisle. That was fear he smelled, right? She didn't look upset, almost looked like she was having an intimate moment with a lover. Were his instincts off? Was this her boyfriend?

Fighting the animal inside, he went to the wall of nighties and browsed through the selection, listening in on their hushed conversation.

"It's time you stop this nonsense and come home to me."

"Aldar, my home is here." Had there been a crack in her voice? He could practically hear the flutter of her rapid heartbeat, not unlike a bird caught in a cage.

"Your home is with me, by my side. As was planned from the start. Why do you continue to avoid your destiny and purpose?"

"Why must my purpose be designed by the males in my life?" Her fists were clenched and lowered at her side. She was shaking, but perhaps with slightly more anger than fear. A step back, shrugging her shoulder back from the man's lips. The movement caused her to look up and make eye contact with Sam over the man's shoulder, and what he saw in their depths triggered him. Panic, longing, a direct question to his soul he was compelled to respond to. He was no longer in control of himself, the beast inside came out. Her look went from pleading to fear in seconds. By the time he put his hand on the man's shoulder and pulled him back from her, the claws and teeth had come out, and he was holding on to the rest of his change by a thread.

"The lady said her home is here, Al." Sam's voice startled her. He didn't need to look in the nearby mirror to see what he looked like. He knew. He hoped that today was a slow day for her, they didn't need any customers walking in on what was happening. On the version of himself he had become. The sinewy man tensed and turned around slowly.

Looking into the eyes of the predator was either very brave or insanely stupid. From the looks of this guy, he was going with the latter.

"This is not your concern, my friend." The man's nostrils flared, as if he had just caught the scent of something distasteful. Arrogance seeped from his pores, as did aristocracy and privilege. The man was classically handsome and built as if he knew his way around a fight, but Sam didn't need to know any more than the fact that Tasha wasn't comfortable to instantly dislike him.

His eyes glanced to Aldar's ears, elongated and topped with points indicative of the Fae race. He hadn't sensed his otherworldliness when he entered. Was Sam losing his edge, or was this man masking himself? Sam didn't care if it made him like his father, this particular elf had to go. Sam gripped his neck and pushed him against the nearest wall. The throb of Aldar's quickened heartbeat pulsed below his palm. He had his attention. Tasha moved warily to the front door then locked it, flipping the sign to indicate she would be back in 10 minutes. It would take him less than five to get rid of this garbage.

"That's where you're mistaken. She is 100% my concern and you and I aren't friends. You have exactly one minute to apologize to her and say your goodbyes." He lowered his head to the Elf's neck, there was no mistaking it now. The scent of the elf's fear finally overpowered his magic. In addition, his core scent had a putrid undertone Sam couldn't help but lock in his primal memory with the other threats. He drew in a long breath, making a point to growl softly as he did it. "You come within miles of this city, you're as good as dead. I never forget a scent," he whispered. "You ever send anyone here to look for her, I'll know. If you ever leave Wisteria again, I'll be told."

He loosened his grip and let Aldar's feet hit the ground. The intruder rubbed his neck as he walked past Tasha, barely giving her a glance. He muttered his comment as he flipped the latch on the door and opened it. "Damaged goods aren't worth the trouble. You'll regret it, shifter." The last word included a tone Sam promised himself he would revisit. Instantly regretting he didn't take care of the trash, Sam started to follow him out the door but was stopped by a delicate hand and a single word.

"Don't."

Her touch centered him. He looked down at her hand and covered it with his own. They watched together as the claws receded, and his hands turned back to human. She looked up at him, and when their eyes met, she finished her thought. "He's not worth it. It's why I left him so long ago."

"I would argue that it would be worth it for me, but I won't do anything you aren't comfortable with. I will let you know that I have no problem tracking him back to Wisteria and beating his ass within an inch of his life."

"I can tell from the way your heart is beating," Tasha whispered. She shook her head and paused, before slipping her hand from beneath his and taking a step back. By the time she looked him in the eye, he had changed back to the man she knew. But instead of admiration, there was hesitancy. He watched as her gaze turned to an apology, and tears formed. She shrugged and shook her head. He hardly registered the next whispered phrase. "This complicates things."

As much as everything in his body was urging him to take her in his arms and never let go, he fought it. The logical part of his brain knew she didn't want it, at least not from him, and not in this moment. He needed to fight the wolf, but his instinct to protect her was almost impossible to overcome. "I didn't know how to tell you."

She continued to shake her head. "For starters, you could have mentioned you researched wolves in fairy tales because you were one." Her voice had gained strength on the last two words. As glad as he was to see her regain her spunk, he wasn't thrilled she was using it against him.

"Tasha, I'm so sorry. Things between us escalated so quickly, and I..."

"Broke your phone? Had better options come along..."

"That's not it. It was dumb of me not to call. I was on my way over just now to tell you that. And then when I got here, it wasn't clear at first what I was walking into. I thought maybe I had gotten my signals crossed."

"I can see that." She nodded. "I'm sorry, I shouldn't put it all on you. You're right. And there was no reason I couldn't have called you. Thank you, by the way, for what you said."

"You're welcome. I meant every word. He'll never get near you again."

"He'll send others, and then I'll have a decision to make that I've been avoiding for a long time."

Sam took a step toward her and then another, until he was close enough to draw her in. She needed the hug, he couldn't watch her attempts to self-soothe anymore. "Have I mentioned how good wolves are at tracking? Scents are a funny thing. They layer themselves on things they are near or things that are touched. I'll know if anyone is sent by him."

"You won't always be around."

He pulled back and cupped her face, tipping it to look into her eyes. The next statement he heard whispered from his lips was unexpected, but the truest thing he ever uttered. "I easily could be, you just need to say the word."

"I know about your kind," she said as the tears fell. "While I was sheltered and never allowed to leave my lands, I did hear stories. I fear that this pull between us is no better than having a choice of who you will marry made for you. I left Wisteria for that very reason. Aldar is my betrothed. It was a human, and the Jinni who introduced us, who ultimately rescued me."

"And where is this man now?" Sam felt her pain as the wound of her sorrow opened, and she allowed it to air.

She calmed herself enough to answer. "He died a long time ago. I've been moving ever since. I had hoped New York would be my last home. It's why my store is named what it is." The tears had slowed.

It was time to be honest with her. "I didn't want anything to do with being an Alpha. I came here with the intent of being an author and living in solitude. I'm not sure what happened, what triggered the change in me causing us to find one another, but now that it's happened, I'm honestly okay with seeing where it leads."

"I'm not sure I can do that. Having things pre-destined, chosen for me, just doesn't sit well."

"I know that better than anyone," he laughed. "I followed my heart, but ultimately, it led me to you. Now the choice is yours, just how far you want to take this. I'm going to do something completely against my nature right now and walk away. But I want you to know that it's not because I don't want you in my life, but because I do. I know you enough to know you need time to decide."

She lifted up on her toes and kissed his cheek. "Thank you, Sam. You're a good man."

He nodded then went to the door. Looking back one more time, he gave her an encouraging smile. "No matter what you decide, I will always be here for you. You know where to find me."

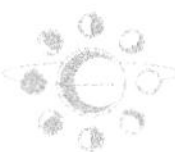

Each step he took in the opposite direction caused his internal beast to howl in pain. The best he could do was swallow the agony… The whiskey helped that night. Finishing his book helped for several nights after. The distractions worked until he dreamed of her, which was every time he slept. For the next full moon cycle, the ropes were replaced with locks and chains. Thankfully, he remained securely fastened until the dawn on those nights. As time went on, hope that he would see her again had waned. He expressed his love for her in the only way he could. He wrote.

9
NATASHA

It had been a few months since she let Sam walk out of her life, but there hadn't been a day that had gone by that she didn't think of him and what a huge mistake that was. She couldn't get him out of her mind, when she received the Author Review Copy from his publisher, she was happy to see that he couldn't get her out of his either. Damn if she didn't want to call him the night she got to the scene in the lingerie store he wrote, which described in intimate detail what the couple was doing near the panty display. To be memorialized in his book was one of the hottest things she'd ever had happen.

He had told her, if she truly wanted to know him, that she only needed to read him. That a piece of him was in everything he wrote and that the wolf stories, especially, included his hopes and dreams. She had read everything he had written with new eyes. In this last book, something shifted in his style, and he had dug deeper with his characters. It had depth and heart, and it had everything to do with meeting her. She could see that now.

Relationships between Lycans and Elvenkind weren't unheard of but were frowned upon by those like her father and ex. Many of the couples who fell in love back home with those outside their kind were forced to leave because of it. She had been one of them. But she and Sam didn't have those same restrictions here. And while she worried about some of the things that affected Lycans when it came to mating and full moons, it was only because she didn't fully understand their world or how they moved within it. There was no better teacher in her mind than the wolf of her heart. She was willing to learn, if he was willing to teach her, she just needed to find out if that was still the case.

She put the final touches on her makeup then slipped on the heels that matched her red dress. They were new and extremely uncomfortable, but if things went well, she wouldn't have them on long. She rolled on some of the lavender essentials from her store display, in an attempt to hide her signature scent. The pages of the book had clued her in once again, and she didn't want to give him any warning she was on her way.

Alice texted her to let her know the last of the customers had left from the signing, and that Sam was packing up for the night. After locking her store, Tasha walked the short distance to the bookstore and waved at Alice through the glass door. Her friend unlocked it and let her slide through before handing her the keys, giving her a quick hug, and a thumbs up. When she mouthed the words "holy goddess, he's hot," Tasha almost snorted. She shook her head at her friend's antics outside the shop's glass door. The shade was pulled down while Alice pointed toward the place where Sam stood and mouthed the word "brother" while waggling her eyebrows as she pointed to herself. Her wink was the last thing Tasha saw before locking the door behind her.

Now…to see where she and Sam stood. His head was down as he packed up what was left of his latest release, the exact one she carried in with her. "I'm almost done here. I'll be out of your hair in a couple minutes."

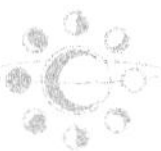

He mistook her for Alice, wearing her friend's favorite scent had worked. From her vantage point on the other side of the shelves, she saw his head lift along with his nose through the small space above the books. He drew in a breath and cocked his head. He placed the books he had been packing away back down on the table, and his stance stiffened. On second thought, maybe it hadn't. Another breath, deeper this time, then he closed his eyes and smiled.

"What if I like you in my hair?" She whispered. He was already moving. "According to this book, you want me in all sorts of places."

He was at the end of the row, hands on either side and his hungry gaze roaming over her. Based on the look in his eyes, the red dress was the right call.

"So, you read page 69?"

"I did. Three times." Her reply was muffled by the stacks that surrounded them. By the sheer power of his predatory nature. His size as it filled the small space wasn't intimidating, but the complete opposite. She fought the urge to throw herself into his arms.

"What did you think?" He took two more strides and closed the gap between them. He lifted a lock of hair that had fallen from her messy bun and rubbed it between his fingers. Happy she wore her hair up, she leaned into the touch he soothed along her ears. Letting someone else in on the secrets she kept was both terrifying and exhilarating.

"I think I was completely insane to let you walk away that day. But it gave me some time to do some research."

The admission lit his face. "And what did you find out?"

"That you are perfect for me." Her body hadn't forgotten, had merely slipped into dormancy in the time they were apart. But it rose to the occasion and reacted to him full force. That he could stoke the flames of her desire with a mere gaze was something she would happily bear for an eternity.

He brushed the tip of his nose against hers then tipped his head to snuggle closer into her neck. "So basically, confirming what I already know?"

She tipped her head to allow him access. "Precisely."

"I'm really glad to hear you say that. Especially considering what happens on page 198." His hands were already sliding up under the skirt of her dress and paused when he brushed across the confirmation that she read his book. "You wore them." He whispered.

"I believe you ordered black?" She turned her back to him and placed her hands on the end display popping her hips out behind her and wiggling her fanny.

His palms were warm on her skin, the pads of his thumbs massaging small circles along the fronts of her thighs, just under the satin straps of her garters.

She glanced over her shoulder with a grin. "Ready for page 271?"

He looked behind him into the darkened room then back into her face with realization. They were blissfully alone. Within seconds, one hand slipped under the tiny triangle of black satin while the other cupped her breast. He lowered his mouth to the crook of her neck; his question was asked between laps of his tongue. "When will your friend be back?"

She paused her answer as his finger slid into her, and she leaned to put his pressure at the perfect angle. Her response was breathy. "We have all night." She thanked the Goddess for that.

The response caused a rumble in his chest, something she could feel more than she could hear. "My prayer was answered. Now all I need is for you to scream my name, love."

Before she could respond, he spun her around and dropped to his knees. Her hips leaned back on the end display, which she used to brace herself as he slipped under her skirt and slid her thong aside. It didn't take long for her to scream his name or for him to howl hers. And in the early morning, when they slipped into the entrance of his apartment, they found other areas of note to make love in, all to be included in the story of their life…together.

EPILOGUE

The new chime Sam had installed on the door sounded out, as the sultry female customer sauntered in. Her thick black hair hung long with loose curls on either side of an above average chest, made more impressive by a cinch-style corset. Tasha loved the bohemian style, even wore it at times, but never looked as fabulous as this customer did doing it. She was glad Sam was at home, not that he would ever stray. They had already had that conversation, and both knew where the other stood.

"Can I help you?" The woman looked like she was here for something in particular. Perhaps earrings to match her emerald necklace? She watched as she eyed the display then pointed to the one on her counter. "If you don't see what you are looking for there, I have some pieces that just came in over here."

The woman smiled and nodded in response, before walking to the display Tasha had pointed out. So, she was looking for jewelry. "Are you looking for something to go with your necklace? That is beautiful, by the way."

Her smile was stunning, and her eyes warmed at the compliment. "Thank you. It was a gift from my husband, although we were dating at the time."

"He has good taste."

"I agree. He picked me after all," the woman laughed. "I hope someone thinks you taste good as well."

Odd way to put it, it almost made her choke on her sip of water. Strangely, she found herself sharing more than she normally would with a stranger. "There is someone. We met a few months ago."

The woman nodded. "I know."

"Excuse me?"

The woman was still smiling, and her eyes were… were they sparkling? Tasha watched as they swirled, like green and golden kaleidoscopes of glitter. The words came to her slowly. "What I mean to say is that you are destined."

"Destined."

Tasha made an attempt but couldn't look away. The last thing her mind did before shutting off completely was call out to Sam.

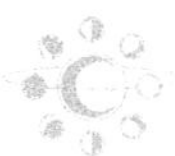

"That's right, my dear." The woman stepped over and helped the woozy Elf into a nearby chair and clicked the stopwatch on her phone. "We will just wait right here for him, it shouldn't take long." It read 3:69.69 when the door chimed and slammed into the wall of the entry. She was holding a pair of emerald-green panties in one hand and pointed a long, lacquered nail toward the counter with the other. "She's fine, darling. Just taking a little nap."

He rolled his eyes. "I'll deal with you in a minute." Slipping to one knee, he took the clerk's pale hand into his and gave it a squeeze. "Tasha, love. Wake up, baby."

"Natasha's a lovely name."

"Not now, Zilla." He tapped Tasha on the cheek and shook his head in disbelief. "I can't believe I didn't put two and two together."

"Black cats are everywhere, darling. But even so, you've been away for some time."

"That was by design."

"And so is this."

"Meaning?" Before Zilla could respond, Tasha started to stir.

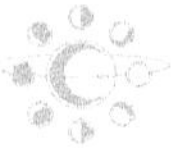

The voices were clearer now. Less muffled and more words. Tasha felt Sam's warm hands over hers, and a sense of relief washed over her. The last memory she had was that of calling out to him, and she was happy to see that their practice had been paying off. Their connection was getting stronger by the day.

"Sam, I didn't want to worry you but started to feel really odd…"

He held a bottle of water up for her. "You can call out to me anytime. Here, drink this."

The water soothed the dryness of her throat. As she drank, he kept glancing to the woman still standing in her showroom.

She was no longer browsing, merely observing her and Sam's interactions.

After the prompting of one more sip, Sam took Natasha's hands in his and pulled her up from the floor to stand. He stood with his back to the showroom, sheltering Tasha from the woman's view as he addressed her. "Are you okay?"

Tasha nodded as Sam looked into her eyes, judging for himself as to her sincerity. As if satisfied with what he saw there, he kissed her forehead and pulled her into his arms, giving her a quick hug before addressing the woman who was already walking toward them.

"Zilla, I would like you to meet Tasha. Tasha, this is Zilla. She's visiting here from Wisteria."

Zilla held out her hand for a handshake. "It's wonderful to meet you properly. I'm glad I finally made the trip here in person, I've been buying from your online store for years."

"Thank you so much," Tasha said genuinely. She had the distinct feeling that this was no ordinary customer, not only by way of where she came from but also Sam's attitude toward her.

"Tell us why you're here, Zilla," Sam said with irritation.

"Well, since we're dispensing with the niceties, I'll get to it. You're both needed back in Wisteria to deal with a situation."

"We both left for a reason."

"Trust me, I know better than anyone that often Fate gets in the middle of what we want and what is needed. As much as you don't care for me, you know I wouldn't be here if it wasn't important. I'll meet you at Sera and Logan's place in a week."

She snapped her fingers, and the air behind her pulled open. The circular shape was rimmed with electric light, and the center reflected an image of the land which Tasha had once called home. In seconds, the woman was gone, and a black cat stood in her place. She knew the woman and shifter were one in the same, there was no denying the eyes which gave Tasha a wink. No sooner had she cleared the portal than the opening disappeared with a snap.

"What was that all about?"

Sam looked at her, cupped her cheeks, and gave her a loving kiss. "I guess we'll be finding out. Ready to go home?"

"I'm already there. It's wherever you are."

To my GDRW writers & friends,
this story wouldn't have been possible without your love and support. Thank you for holding the light as I traveled through the darkness and for your continued faith in me. You were right... I could find my way back to the keyboard.

A SHIFTER FOR SOLSTICE

Can a reluctant Alpha find a new beginning at his older brother's wedding?

A one-night stand turns into more when a werewolf learns the sexy bookworm he had in his arms is the Maid of Honor in his brother's wedding—the same brother who turned his back on the pack, left him in charge, and hasn't shared his true identity with anyone.

1
BRENT

Lavender and Sun-kissed skin. A floral musk which was distinctly feminine. The scent was stronger here in New York and something that had been driving him insane since he had arrived through the portal near his brother's apartment. He had imprinted on it unwilling…stubborn. His mind couldn't help it; the magick wove through his senses. With each step he took to his destination the fragrance grew thicker. When she walked into the room, he understood why.

Brent Randall had been about to leave when she entered the bar. She was dressed casually, her long, auburn hair pulled up in a messy bun and sparkly cat-eyeglasses perched mid-nose. Perhaps she was traveling like he was and staying in the same hotel since she looked like she was committed to the barstool she perched on. At least that was his assumption, considering the size of the half-read book she had in her hand. She was far enough from him that she hadn't noticed him glancing her way but if he didn't stop leaning toward her intoxicating scent, he'd be sure to scare her off. Especially if she caught him sniffing the air like the dog he was related to. The perfume was 20% bottle, and 80% her, he'd bet on it. It was the 80% that had his dick twitching.

She looked content to be alone, preferred it actually, as she ordered another drink from the bartender and thanked him with a dazzling smile before cracking back into the thick tome she had brought with her. He was impressed by her drink choice. Nothing fruity or sweet like he'd expect. Simple, on the rocks, something savored instead of rushed.

Just like the images of sex that were starting to run through his mind.

He was content to sit back and watch her, ordering another drink, even though he had an early morning. He sipped his scotch on the rocks, and watched her do the same, while he contemplated his next move. The man who came into the bar and sat next to her made his choice for him, as did the hairs rising on the back of his neck. Thankfully the full moon was weeks away, but the effects were still messing with his head. A threat was a threat, and a shifter knew one when they sensed one.

Brent watched as the slime set his beefy hand on top of her delicate shoulder. His thumb slid up and down her clavicle making her lean away with every swipe. His paw was much too close to her neck. A neck that Brent was convinced with every passing second belonged to him. Her smile was polite but strained, as if she wanted him to leave but had never been equipped with the proper way to get out of a bad situation. *Punch to the throat, mace in the face, anything but a smile, my Sweet.* Brent didn't miss the intake of her breath or the barely perceived wince as she shrugged her shoulder away from the possessive touch. Her nervous twitter hit his senses like a bullhorn. She wasn't going to tell him to fuck off, so Brent was forced to make his move. He slid between them and removed the ape's hand from her arm faster than the scent of her fear could reach his nose.

The man was irritated but was smart enough to stay seated. "Bug off, Buddy."

"I think the lady would like you to leave." Brent wedged his body further between them forcing the man to shift his stool back slightly. The man didn't have a choice, his only alternative was to be within reach of Brent's grip, one that was pulsing visibly between tight and loose with each intake of breath. He was reigning it in, but between the awareness of her behind him and the desire to punch the jeering face in front of him, he was about to lose control.

"I think the lady wants me to stay. Now take off, I got this."

The man was slurring his words, he must have come from another bar. Brent guessed he had gotten cut off considering how drunk he was. "I'm not sure what you think you've got since the lady seems extremely uncomfortable with you right now."

"I think the lady's just fine, she's smiling."

"I'm smiling too, but that doesn't mean I like you or that I'm going to hold back from fucking you up if you don't keep your hands off her."

"What's it to you, asshole."

If only he was in a dark alley with this trash. "Considering she's my fiancé, I think I have a lot to say about it." From the look on the man's face, Brent realized his eyes must have changed, lit from the inside like the fires of hell. He could feel his anger pooling in the pit of his stomach. The threat was easy to hear in his next sentence. "And if you'd like to have this conversation outside, I'd be happy to do that."

"I'm sure that won't be necessary, Honey." How had she moved so quietly? She was out of her seat and standing by his side with her hand on his arm. Her touch was electric. It almost made him forget what he was so upset about. "I'm ready to go back up to our room."

"I call bullshit." The man made a final desperate attempt to save his pride.

"I have nothing to prove to a scumbag like you, but seeing as though I haven't seen my lady all day…"

Brent placed his hands on either side of her delicate face and looked deep into her eyes for consent. He was counting on her to support his bluff, watching her lick her lips while the lavender from her warm skin soothed his frazzled nerves, he needed it more than his next breath. Her pink sparkly lips parted, arms slid around his neck, and her head tilted back.

"I've missed you, Lover."

The sigh that came from her as his lips touched hers punched him in the gut. And when her delicate tongue reached his it took the breath from his lungs. Bodies clung, hands groped, and he was keeping it together until he felt her hand grip at the back of his shirt just above his ass. Fucking A, what had he done?

"There are places upstairs for that," the bartender called out. "Am I adding this tab to your room?"

When Sam looked up the man was gone. The threat was no longer there, but there was no way he was going to let this night end now.

There was something special about her.

"Room 690. Both tabs," Brent responded.

The bartender nodded, already two steps to the register as he heard a quiet voice say, "I like the number."

He could hardly respond fast enough. "Want to see it?"

Slight hesitation, lowering of her lids, then a straightening of her shoulders and a decisive nod. A decision had been made that had nothing to do with him, but more to do with this moment. If it kept her in his arms a little longer, he would take it.

He gripped her hand before she could change her mind and led her to the wall of elevators. The first set opened as he turned to ask her the one thing, he knew he would regret later if he didn't. "You sure?"

She nudged him through the sliding doors and pushed the button for floor six, then the doors, before cupping her hands on his face and pulling it down to hers. "Absolutely."

The kiss ignited him, and he lifted her legs on either side of him until she crossed and locked them behind his waist. He groaned as the bell chimed for his floor. He didn't put her down, merely carried her the short distance to his room as she planted kisses along his neck and whispered obscenities into his ear. She was too good to be true. The things she was saying she wanted to do to him in no way matched the librarian look she had going on, which was the biggest turn on he had ever had in his life.

A quick key card swipe as she slipped her eyeglasses off, and they were in. She dropped her purse and case to one side and book to the other, then draped them back over his shoulders with a grin. The twinkle in her emerald eyes did him in completely. Glasses or no, they were one of her best features. "Nice room," she whispered. "Way better than my apartment. Must be because you're in it."

"That could be rectified later, but for now we stay here."

"I have nowhere to be until the morning. Until then I'm all yours."

"I'm not sure you realize what that means."

She pushed herself against his hardon and grinned. "I'm a romance reader, I have a pretty good idea."

His laugh erupted before he dove in for another kiss. If he wasn't careful, he would imprint on this saucy minx before the night was over. At the very least, he would never be able to light another lavender candle without thinking of her.

"Are we having sex against this door?" Her hopeful tone had him smiling.

"Do you want sex against this door? I mean, I have a perfectly good bed over there."

She spoke between kisses. "Oh, I want to try that too."

"I'm game. But first…" He lowered her to her feet long enough to unbuckle his pants, slip his wallet from his pocket, and remove a condom before dropping his clothing and the wrapper in a heap.

Her purple lace thong landed on the pile as he slipped on the rubber. She jumped up into his arms again, wiggling against him with a grin.

"I love dresses," he murmured.

"Me too. Almost as much as boxers," she answered.

He adjusted his grip placing one hand on her ass, and the other slipping under the floral print dress which reminded him of the fields back home. His fingers found her core easily as she had her legs wide on either side of his waist and was unable to close them. They gripped him tight as his fingers slipped against her gold causing pants of delighted frustration as she undulated against his hand. He couldn't prevent it from happening, nor did he have any desire to; her essence was branded on his soul.

Her nails dug as he stroked, the moans they shared captured in the frantic kisses which ended when he swallowed her scream and held her trembling body.

He kept two fingers inside her until he felt the slowing of her orgasm, then replaced his fingers with his cock and started the frenzy anew, triggering waves of desire for them both with every shudder of her body. She leaned back, tilting her hips forward, and pressed into every thrust with a breathy groan. It took every bit of resistance he had left to bite back the howl rising to the top of his throat. To claim her with his mark.

They switched positions, and he pressed her against the door with the lower half of his body, his forehead resting against hers. She opened her eyes then and gazed into his, as if gauging the depths of his soul and what she would find, then grinned. The knowing in her eyes sealed his fate.

"You mentioned a bed?"

"I did. Which position should we start in?"

"Dealer's choice," she answered then kissed his nose. "Sweetheart."

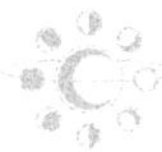

He couldn't get her on his bed quick enough. In that moment he knew pretending to be engaged for the night then going their separate ways the next day wouldn't cut it. But by the morning he realized it would have to be because she had left without a word. The only confirmation he had that he hadn't dreamed the entire thing, was the tiny scrap of lavender lace that lay on top of his pile of clothes, and the six condom wrappers that littered the floor.

Brent had been engaged, even lied about finding his mate so his brother would leave home and chase his dreams, but never fully embraced his duties as Alpha. It wasn't something he had ever wanted, neither had Sam, but where did that leave their pack? He had come to town fully intending to have the discussion with Sam now that he was settling down with Tasha, but this feeling he had, like half of his soul had been stolen from his body and stuffed into the canvas book tote she had carried, had him questioning himself. Was there something to this whole mate thing? Sweaty palms, racing heart, and shallow breath. Or maybe he was just coming down with something?

He had seen the crazed effects of mating and had wanted nothing to do with it. Faked it even. He had done the Alpha thing for years, but only for his brother. He wanted his own life, to follow his own dreams, but if this pull he felt for his mystery lady was real, if it kept her in his arms until the unforeseeable future, perhaps he was willing to give it a try. He had known her less than a few hours and he was already obsessed. He needed answers only another shifter could give him, and he couldn't put off the inevitable conversation. But first, he needed to shower. He had a wedding rehearsal to get ready for and a brother to disappoint.

2.
ALICE

Alice felt like shit sneaking out like a thief at 4:00 AM, but she had a spa day to get ready for and she needed a shower. Bad. There was no way she would take one there since she was confident it would have led to another round, and she was pretty sure he had run out of condoms. Not to mention, she could hardly move. How she was going to pull off 3-inch heels at the wedding the next day was a mystery.

A sign of contentment passed through her puffy lips. She pulled in a breath, sandalwood and sex. It was the first scent of man covering her body in months. Her body ached in all the right places, which wasn't surprising since she had been bent into every sexual position known to man...and some that weren't. He had surprised even her and considering she owned a bookstore and read every book on the subject they carried, that wasn't easy. It was hands down the most amazing sex she had in her life, and she had never had that much fun making love before. It was easy, carefree, intimate, and joyful. That was the word. The laughter they shared caused the joy to bubble up from her soul. Their connection, profound. Her intent was to remain nameless to him, to never see him again, but now she was second-guessing that decision. What if he had been the one?

Tommy hadn't been. Due to a spell that was a bit more powerful than she had probably needed at the time, they had broken up and he had left town a year before. She didn't know at the time it would be months of a sex drought without him, and she had just started to lose hope she would ever be attracted to anyone ever again when the Universe dropped her mystery man at the end of the hotel bar. How she longed at the time to be the ice cubes in his glass.

She had noticed him looking, liked the way he sipped his Scotch, and smoothed his trimmed beard with his muscular hands. The dark hair suited him, as did the smoldering eyes, and he had the bonus of a broad set of shoulders and tapered waist. She found out later that the dress shirt was hiding rock-hard abs sprinkled with just the right amount of dark hair trailing down to a glorious… the horn honked, and she stepped back onto the curb. She really needed to focus. Perhaps when she got home, she would be better off with a cold shower for her libido instead of the warm one she had planned for her muscles.

Her cell chimed, a text from her friend, Tasha.

You stopped texting last night, all okay?

Alice looked through her messages from the night before. Tasha had been concerned.

I'm good. Better than good. Amazing. Will chat about it when I see you. Need a shower.

You got laid, didn't you?

:)

About time! See you soon.

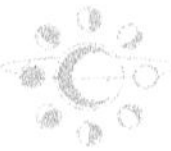

It didn't take her long to get ready since they were lined up for a day of pampering and would be getting facials anyway. She took extra time in the shower, then wore her hair pulled up in her signature clip and slipped into some yoga pants and a large tee. Her face was makeup free and she slipped her feet into flip flops in preparation for the pedicure they were starting with. Tasha was already soaking her feet when Alice came into the room and was ushered to the massage chair next to her.

"So…" she smiled. "How was your date?"

Alice blushed. "No date, just mind-blowing sex."

Tasha gasped playfully. "Alice Leto! You naughty thing! Well... dish!"

"He came to my rescue at the hotel up the street from our shops. I had stopped there to shake off the day. Some guy was getting grabby, and my hero wasn't having it. So, he pretended to be my fiancé."

"And you thanked him for being your pretend fiancé by having real sex with him?" Tasha was sitting up in her seat now.

"Exactly," Alice laughed. "Don't give me that look, you know how long it's been for me. I needed to make sure it all still worked."

"And did it?"

"And then some, although I'm not sure it will ever be the same. I had no idea it could be like that, Tasha."

"Well, it definitely can and should be. I'm glad you're okay. You know, I was a little worried."

"I know you were, I'm sorry," Alice said. "Things just happened so fast, and before I knew it, I was in his room for the night. By the time I left it was late. Well, technically early."

"Walk of shame! You go! But you know it's never too late to reach out to me."

"Thanks." Alice put her feet in the filled tub to soak. "You know, I wouldn't have done that with just anyone. There was something really special about him."

That got Tasha's attention. "Something physically special?" She grinned.

"Definitely that too, but no it was something more than that. I knew right away I could trust him. That he would protect me. This might sound crazy, but it felt a lot like some of those books I've been reading."

Alice looked up and caught Tasha's expression which looked like a cross between worry and elation. Or perhaps she imagined it since as soon as she saw it, it was gone.

"What did you say this guy's name was again?"

"Sadly, we didn't exchange them," Alice shrugged. The movement made her wince, her skin was tender. She sat up in the massage chair and clicked off the rollers and heat.

"You, okay?"

"Yes, although I think I may be having a reaction to this new body wash. So irritating, this is the third one I've tried in a month."

"I've been working on something that I hope will do the trick for you." Tasha leaned over and reached her hand out. "In the meantime, I can take a look, lean this way."

Alice bent over the arm of her chair and allowed Tasha to pull up her cotton tee. She was not expecting the gasp.

"Mother, Maid and Crone."

"What?" Alice shot up in her seat and reached up to feel behind her neck. The skin was raised in tiny lines there, which was one of the points of discomfort. Tasha's face registered shock, then she shook it slowly.

"None of my business, my friend, but how rough did it get?"

The comment gave Alice pause. She shook her head as she answered. "Not rough at all, he was sweet and tender. Well, after holding me against the door the first time with his…"

"I get the idea," Tasha laughed.

"He had to have been one of the most considerate lovers I have had in my life. We didn't do anything I wasn't comfortable with."

"As it should be," Tasha said. "Just wanted to check since there are quite a few scratches I can see."

Alice blushed and covered her smirk with her hand. "Well, there were some other pretty unconventional places we…"

Tasha raised her hand, palm forward. "TMI." she shook her head with a smile. "Maybe there were some hard surfaces…"

"I can guarantee there were."

Tasha practically spit out the water she had been drinking. "Thank the Goddess you got laid, had you gone any longer the scratches could have been so much worse."

"Truly." Alice agreed. "Come to think of it, the top of my ass stings a bit. But, so worth it."

"How are you going to pull off your dress in two days?" Tasha shook her head with a grin.

"A shawl and a thong? Maybe just the shawl? Will have to check out my butt."

"Guess we will be heading to my shop at some point, and I will be upping the production on that body butter I'm working on. You will be getting your Solstice gift early."

"This has been my lucky week," Alice said. She thought about the stranger with the mossy hazel eyes and rakish smile and wondered if they had exchanged names and numbers if it would have worked out. Odds were, they wouldn't have, she had sensed player vibes in him, but since she went into it without expectations, she was one with her decision. It might have been a one-night stand, but in those few hours she felt more cherished than she had in the entire relationship with her ex. Hell, with any of her exes. It had been just what she needed to put herself back out there and stop hiding behind the romance novels she sold.

If nothing else, one night with him had made her realize love was out there for her. As much as she liked the way she could lose herself in the fantasy worlds she read about, she needed to be more present. She glanced at her friend who was grinning at the screen on her phone and texting a response. It had to be Sam, there was no other person on the planet that made Tasha beam like that.

Now, to find the person who lit her fire…to give her a happily-ever-after. She was finally open to the possibilities and ready to look for her Mr. Right. Tasha was right; it was about time.

3
BRENT

Brent had been seated at a table in the hotel restaurant when Sam made his way in. He finished the call he was on then gave him a quick hug and pat on the back before sitting in the seat across from him. Sam nodded to the waiter who offered him coffee and poured a creamer in it before taking a sip. They had about an hour together before he had to leave for a meeting with his publisher.

"I feel bad not spending more time with you during your stay. My schedule is cram packed right now. I wish you would have taken me up on staying at the apartment."

"I'm moving there tonight to give us more time together. I knew you had a ton to do and I've been keeping myself busy the past couple of days. Even took in a couple shows, so don't worry about me."

"Appreciate it. For such a small wedding, it's been a lot of work. Trying to keep it intimate for Tasha, but simultaneously appeasing my public relations manager, has been a juggling act. I'll be glad when it's over and we are soaking up some sun in Jamaica."

"I can imagine. Never been there. Wonder if the person you are standing me up with would like to go?"

"Oh no, Tasha's best friend is off limits. Besides, you are already engaged, and she wouldn't be your type even if you weren't."

"Why is that?"

"I don't know her that well, she keeps to herself, but she's a pretty big introvert."

"Nothing wrong with wanting to stay home."

"She reads a ton, brainy type, owns a bookstore down from Tasha's shop."

"I like them smart," Brent answered. "And I do like books."

"True, I guess you do have books in common," Sam nodded. "And she likes witchy stuff, not sure if she practices necessarily, but Tasha has mentioned she has a natural ability that she has picked up on. She's been working with her on some stuff, I stay out of it mostly."

"Never dated a witch, wouldn't mind giving it a try. So, what does she look like? Dark hair?"

"Sort of a reddish color, on the long side, and she wears glasses. Nothing like you normally go after and she certainly isn't anything like your fiancé. Where is Nadia, by the way?"

"She's tied up with family obligations and we decided it would be best if she stayed behind and kept an eye on things."

"I suppose that makes sense," Sam mused. The waiter took their order and topped off their coffees before leaving them to their conversation. "I hate when they do that. Now I will never get the right balance of cream vs coffee in my cup."

"You could have worse problems," Brent laughed. "Like having a life you hate, or a fiancé who doesn't love you."

"True." Thankfully, Sam was responding to a text and only half heard him. "How are things going at home?"

"Fine," Brent answered flatly. He never listened to anything he had to say, even when they were pups.

"Good. I was worried after the altercation with Aldar that issues with the Elves would start up again. Logan's pack is the closest to their lands, he hasn't reported anything to you?"

"No, things have been quiet. He's lending a hand this weekend, as I've done for him when he travels with Sera. It's worked out well for both packs, the members are all open-minded and respond to either authority."

"Really? Interesting. That sure wouldn't have happened back in our grandfather's time."

"Hades, no," Brent agreed. "They would have burned their own village before letting another Alpha take over. It was pretty fucked up."

"Yeah, it still was during Father's time in some areas. I'm glad things have finally leveled out. The toxicity was hard on us all."

"Me too. Having a balance back has been nice, but sometimes I wonder if we could have found another way. If it was worth the price we paid. I miss having you around."

"I miss you too, Brent. Me leaving was for the best though. It worked out as it should, I would have never met Tasha otherwise."

"I know," Brent changed the subject before it went south. "So, when am I meeting this woman I'm coupled with?"

"Tonight, at the rehearsal dinner. You will be sitting with us at a table for four, by the way, she doesn't know about us, who we really are, and Tasha wants to keep it that way for now."

"Why? Doesn't she trust her?"

"No, it isn't that. She trusts her, she is just trying to keep her safe. Tasha is feeling a little more exposed since I'm sort of in the public eye. We are trying to find a balance, but in the meantime, she is super protective of the ones who mean the most to her."

"Understandable. Ever think about coming back to Wisteria?"

Sam shook his head. "Not an option for her, she's made her life here. Since she's my life, I'm here to stay as well." His phone vibrated and Sam looked down, then apologized. "Sorry, need to take this call. I'll be right back."

Brent watched his older brother chat animatedly to someone he presumed was Tasha. The smile on his face was a dead giveaway. How he wished he could follow his own dreams, choose his own responsibilities, and find the love of his life. But in allowing his older brother the freedom to chase his dreams, he closed the door on his own. Now with Tasha in his brother's life, there was no turning back for any of them unless a compromise could be made. He wasn't sure he would want to make one if the tables were turned.

Sam came back to the table in time to pay the tab and apologize for the short visit before heading to his next appointment. Much like Wisteria had needed a few years back, his brother needed some balance. So did he and he wasn't sure he would find it by continuing to carry the burden of his Alpha duties alone. One would argue that was what the Alpha's mate was for, but the trouble was, he was a single Beta and doomed to a bachelor life if the several failed relationships was any indication.

It was time to come up with a solution, but Brent didn't want to approach his brother with his ideas quite yet. Sam had relinquished his Alpha duties, but didn't act like any beta Brent had ever seen. Sam almost flipped his nut about getting his coffee warmed up, what would he say if Brent suggested they share the Alpha duties three ways with Logan? He supposed there was only one way to find out, but it certainly wouldn't be tonight.

He decided to enjoy himself while he was here, and let the cards play out. He was looking forward to meeting Tasha's friend and seeing if she was as prudish as Sam attempted to make her sound. Brent highly doubted it. Perhaps she could help get his mystery woman off his mind. He highly doubted that too.

4
ALICE

Winter in New York was Alice's favorite season. The city was friendlier, and the already stunning visual display was unmatched in any city she had ever traveled to. Her friend picked the perfect time for her wedding. Solstice and a new moon were a great choice for new beginnings especially when you were starting a new life with someone.

Tasha and Sam had decided on an intimate ceremony at the Russian Tea Room, the place near and dear to their hearts since it was the place that represented their first "date." It made Alice wonder if her destined husband would be okay with her choice of location since it was a bit out of the ordinary. The perfect way to tie the knot in her mind was in the woods surrounded by the people you loved. Blanketed by the hush of the trees and bound to the man she loved with two braided cords in a handfasting ceremony, she would choose the witches' New Year and have her ceremony on All Hallows Eve. She liked the idea of bringing in the new year with the man she gave her heart to.

In truth she didn't know much about Tasha's past even though she considered her one of her dearest friends. She was intuitive enough to know she was hiding things from her, but a good enough friend to realize she would share it with her when she was ready. Tasha had been hurt deeply and had trust issues, that was clear enough.

Alice knew even less about the man her friend was marrying, Sam Randall. However, she had read his books and anyone who wrote

Romance with the feeling and heart that he did couldn't be all bad. His fairy tale retellings had been one of the best-selling books for her to date. Now that he was dating her bestie, the events at her shop had increased and so had the revenue. His latest book *Phoenix* had just gone viral on social media, and she couldn't keep it on the shelves.

"I think that is it for the favors," Tasha said. "The centerpieces look great, don't they?"

Alice nodded. "They really do. Who knew a book could look so good. Sam will be excited to see we put his proof copies to such good use."

"I love these bookmarks you made with the pages, by the way. His publicist will go mad for these."

"Good thing I didn't need to make more than 50 of them," Alice laughed. "They were sort of a pain in the ass."

Her friend made eye contact with her, and they shared a grin. The next sentence was stated deadpan in unison. "Like most men."

They laughed, then Alice added, "Except for Sam, of course. You got a good one."

Tasha's expression was like it always was when they spoke of her future husband, thoughtful and starry-eyed.

"I did, didn't I? It only took forever."

"I know what you mean," Alice murmured. "So, is this it? Any more to set up?"

Tasha shook her head. "No, I have Jasmine lined up to do the rest so we can go get dressed. Let's head to my shop now so we can get back in time for a quick drink before the guests arrive."

Alice followed her out the door and they walked down to Roots which was just up the street from her bookstore, Turn the Page. Years before, their grand openings were within a month of each other, so they had done a ton of cooperative ads together at the time. They had been fast friends ever since.

"I have to show you this set I have for tomorrow night. It's a surprise for Sam."

Tasha unlocked the door and ushered Alice in before closing and locking the door behind them. Alice was already walking over to the new arrivals by the time Tasha flicked the lights on.

"Oh Tasha, this is gorgeous!" Holding two diamond straps on her shoulders, the shimmery lavender and aubergine fabric slipped across her stomach stopping at mid-thigh. The pattern looked very much like a distant constellation, magical and sparkly.

"That would look amazing on you with your coloring. I'm sure I have it in your size."

"I'll take it," Alice gushed. "I've always wanted a nightie like this, and Tommy never picked up on the hint to get me one. I'm going to treat myself. It's stunning."

"Consider it a Bridesmaid gift," Tasha said as she handed a tissue filled bag to Alice. "Who knows, maybe your mystery man will be the first to see you in it."

"If only," Alice gushed. "Not sure that will happen, honestly, not sure I want it to. I was a little on the uninhibited side with him and he may have gotten the wrong idea about me."

Tasha nodded and pursed her lips, her perfectly manicured finger tapping them as if deep in thought. "I mean, I get it, my friend. But sometimes you need to get past the fear to get to the good stuff. Someone who you are meant to be with needs to love you for who you are."

"I know. I'm just tired of getting hurt after they get to know who I really am."

"I get it, I really do." Tasha gave her a quick hug which caused the welling tears to roll. "Sam and I had our moments, as you well know."

"I remember," Alice nodded. "I don't consider myself in the same crazy stalker ex-boyfriend category though. You had a way better excuse for hiding from love and turning your heart against it after you shared what happened. He's lucky he didn't end up in jail."

"I mean my ex was something, but I don't agree," Tasha said as she tossed a few more pieces of lingerie at Alice from a nearby display. "Hiding from love for fear of wasting any more of your time is sometimes the best thing you can do for yourself. It gives your heart a chance to align and attract the right person for you."

"Sort of like the spells I've been working on?"

"Exactly."

"What are these for?" Alice questioned as she held up the lacey thong and matching bralette Tasha had given her.

"Just one more thing to align your heart and mind with what you truly want. You want mind-blowing sex with the perfect man for you? Time to start dressing for him and empowering yourself."

Alice looked down at the lavender lacies and blushed. "Well, I do need two new pair of these since I seemed to have misplaced the ones I bought here last week."

Tasha grinned. "See, it's working already. Magick panties."

"Coincidence," Alice muttered as she followed her friend back to the changing rooms.

"Hate to tell you, but nothing is a coincidence, it is always by design. Fate always gets her way; I know that from experience. Best thing to do is to be prepared for her when it happens."

"What if it never happens?"

"Oh, it will," Tasha said from the stall next to hers. "And when it does, you will look fabulous."

Alice looked at the image staring back at her, then twisted to look at her ass. Scratches and all, Tasha was right, she did look fabulous. The lavender thong was just the thing she needed to complete her outfit for the wedding. The underwire pushup she had special ordered would work perfectly under her embellished A-line dress. The last thong she had didn't last long in his hands and it made her wonder how long she would stay in anything with him around. It made her sad he wouldn't see her in it and hoped the next man Fate brought into her life liked purple. It was her signature color.

"What do you think?" Tasha's voice questioned from the other stall. A question with more than one answer, but Alice answered the one she knew her friend intended.

"I think Fate better get ready for me."

"Now we're talking." Tasha pulled the curtain open and stood in the opening decked out in a gauzy chiffon baby doll in ivory with threads of gold which practically made it glow. The contrast with Tasha's dark hair and eyes was striking.

"You look positively ethereal, like a star brought to life. Sam is one lucky man, my friend."

Tasha blushed prettily, and at that moment she was so grateful to Sam for bringing love into Tasha's life. It gave her hope that it was out there for her as well. "Thanks, Alice. That means a lot." She glanced at her watch and rushed back to her own dressing room. "We had better get moving, he's always early."

"They say opposites attract," Alice joked as she changed into her rehearsal dinner outfit.

"Very funny," Tasha laughed.

The friends chatted while applying their makeup and finishing their hair. The final touch before leaving the store was a dab of essential oil from Tasha's display.

"I have a new shipment coming in next week. Your lavender is in that order, but I tucked the sample bottle behind the counter. It has a bit left in it."

"Thanks for ordering for me, I'm almost out. The shop has been much busier with the holidays, and I find having it going in the diffuser helps everyone's stress levels, including mine."

"Yeah, works great here as well with the sage I burn. It's soothing."

They walked out and Tasha locked up, then the two of them made their way up the street toward the Tea Room. Thankfully it hadn't snowed, so their walk was quicker. They made it back to the restaurant with 20 minutes to spare, and Sam was already at the bar chatting to Jasmine. His smile lit the room when he saw Tasha and as the two embraced Alice couldn't help but feel a tiny bit jealous. Sam was the perfect man, gorgeous, successful, and a romance author to boot. It didn't hurt that Tasha was the sun in his orbit, you only had to look at the way he looked at her. If only she could find the same.

Maybe there was something to be said about Fate. Maybe she should have helped her along by leaving Mystery Man her number. Now she would never know if it could have been more. Perhaps it was time to start taking matters into her own hands. The banishment spell had worked on Tommy, who was to say she couldn't weave a love spell just as powerful.

"I have your drinks right here, ladies."

"Thanks, Sam." Alice raised her glass of scotch to Jasmine and acknowledged her with a nod. Holding it in front of her, the couple followed suit. "To the best friend a girl could ask for, and the man who captured her heart. I wish you both all the happiness in the world."

"Thank you, cheers to that," Tasha said as they all clinked glasses and took a sip.

"If only you had a brother," Alice joked. She took another sip of her scotch as she caught movement in her peripheral.

"I do. Younger by a year," Sam smiled. "Although, he's taken. Oh, here he is now."

The scotch she had just sipped was dangerously close to being spat out, as the man she had seen naked just this morning locked gazes with her and made his way over. A flush rose from her stomach to her face and it wasn't from the alcohol. She was processing everything at once, the way he looked in a suit, the fact that the stubble on his chin that had rubbed her skin raw was gone, that he was TAKEN! Fuck! What had she done?

At first there was surprise on his face, then confusion. He read the room as she frantically sipped her drink and avoided his direct gaze. He shifted his direction at the last minute and walked up to his brother first, giving Sam a bear-hug and hitting him on the back. Alice had a ton of emotions brewing inside, touched by the sentimental display.

Tasha hugged him next, quickly and not nearly as closely. By the straight back and the space between their bodies, Alice surmised that they didn't know one another well. That and she was skittish around men, overall. Sam was the only one who didn't bring out the defensiveness in her.

Sam turned with his brother to face Alice who was frantically trying to disappear into her tumbler of Dewars. Too bad the portrait of Felix the Cat didn't include his famous bag of tricks; she would attempt to slip into that if she could. He was waiting… staring… she had no choice but to lift her head and make eye contact with the man who had been circling her thoughts every hour on the hour since she had slipped from his bed.

"This is Alice," Sam introduced. "Tasha's Maid of Honor and best friend. Alice, this is my brother, Brent. Also, my Best Man."

Thankfully, he put his hand out and took hers as she offered it. He murmured "nice to meet you" as he lifted it to his lips with a grin. His eyes had the same twinkle, his mouth the dimple she was obsessed with to the left of the lips he caressed her with in more places than she could think about now. He and Sam were practically twins, but her nipples never reacted the way they did when Sam said the next word that rumbled from Brent's lips.

"Alice."

Did he just inhale her scent before kissing the back of her fingers? Oh, Mother goddess was that his tongue? He was slow to raise his head, and she held her breath as he winked and gave her hand a squeeze.

"Looks like we will be spending a couple nights together," he said with a grin. "Very nice to meet you."

Alice swallowed and barely squeaked out a response. "Nice to meet you too." Tasha placed her hand on Alice's elbow, concern in her eyes. Alice gave a subtle shake of her head and took a deep breath. "Let's get you a drink." The smile felt forced, her walk stiff, as she ordered an Ivan the Terrible from Jasmine since everyone needed to enjoy at least one signature drink from The Russian Tea Room during their visit. Next to scotch, it was her go-to order here, so she knew he would like it. That she already knew his preference unnerved her.

As she handed him his drink, the look in his eyes did her in. He was enjoying her discomfort, or perhaps curious about it. What was wrong with him? Shouldn't he be embarrassed? He looked anything but. Speaking of butts, hers still stung and she looked at his hands wrapped around the glass he lifted to his lips. Perfectly manicured. Ugh, was there anything about this man that wasn't perfect? Oh yeah… he was TAKEN!

Alice had reached a new low in her opinion; she had slept with another woman's man. But the thing that was making her queasy like too many Cosmopolitans on an empty stomach was the fact that if she had the choice to do it all over again…she would consider it. I mean, Mother Goddess, just look at him! What did that say about her?

She slammed the rest of her drink and nodded to Jasmine for another. Sam and Tasha were already greeting guests and didn't notice her edginess. Alcohol wasn't ever the answer, but she hadn't put her scent chamber on and didn't have her smudge. As she raised her glass to her lips, she glanced over to the couple who were now introducing Brent to the team in charge of Sam's book production. His shoulders were broad, his suit perfectly tailored. Sip. The feel of his lips still warmed the back of her hand like a brand. Sip. His laugh was soothing, his scent unbelievingly wafting up to her from her skin. Sip. Was it hot in here or was it just him?

It was time to get some air.

5
ALICE

lice needed to ground. At her request the introductions didn't include her and the guests who had arrived were already seated and chatting with the people at their tables. With each sentence she overheard, her feet shifted closer to the door. Soon she was following them through the main entrance and out onto West 57th Street.

The night was mild considering the winter solstice was just a day away. Her sheer scarf and bulky sweater were enough with the radiant heat of the concrete; besides she didn't plan to be long. She had no idea where she was going and tripped over a small black cat in her haste. The poor thing hissed and swatted at her bare ankles, then acted as if it was going to launch itself at her. It caused Alice to turn in the other direction and quicken her steps to avoid its wrath.

Soon enough, her feet were leading her to Central Park, to her favorite place along the path. The arrival of the man she knew in all the ways that didn't matter in polite conversation, had her energy spiraling in all directions. The fresh air was already calming her, it had been the right call and Tasha knew her well enough to know she wandered off from time to time to regulate her anxiety.

She traveled past the hot dog cart she and Tasha frequented and gave Ernie a wave, before heading through the small concrete tunnel to her favorite bench on the other side. It was far enough off the street to hear the trees, but close enough to Ernie's stand to feel safe. Her lungs filled with the crisp night air laced with the scent of roasting frankfurters, sauerkraut, and dried leaves. The snow hadn't started, but it was close. She could smell that as well, a heavy dampness with a hint of fresh linen. If only it were warmer, she would have her shoes kicked off and toes in the grass to add one more layer to her session. The scents and sounds that always comforted her would have to be enough for tonight.

The night was just starting to soothe her jangled nerves as she registered the footsteps. She slipped her hand in her pocket around the slim black container she always carried and flipped the switch with her thumb. The steps of the shadow moving toward her were weighted and strode with purpose, most likely they would pass her quickly, but she never took her chances. The shadow was wide, definitely male from the way it moved. She calculated the odds of making it past him and through the tunnel without him getting close enough to her, but he was moving too fast. His head was locked forward, never searching his surroundings, as if he had one goal in mind. Trouble was he was heading right toward her… spray in the face it would be then.

She pushed her glasses up to the bridge of her nose then lifted the pepper spray just as the ambient light hit Brent's features. Lowering the container, she sighed in relief.

"You scared the crap out of me," she said as she flipped the lock on the cylinder and slipped it back into her sweater pocket.

"I could say the same," Brent quipped. "What were you thinking wandering off alone?"

Alice scrunched her face, a question laced with irritation she hoped he could see. "I live here," she responded with a snap. "I'm down here all the time." Another push on her glasses caused her to regret missing her optometry appointment in all the chaos. She really needed to get them looked at.

Brent paced in front of her, his agitation with her stressing her even more than his presence.

"Will you please sit? You are making me nervous."

"I'm the least threatening thing within a 2-mile radius, especially when it comes to you," Brent answered. She didn't understand why he was so worked up, the swipe of his hand down his face, and deep breath, caused her to pause. Had he been worried?

"A two-mile radius is specific. And considering I just met you; how could I possibly know that? It seems there are a lot of things we don't know about one another."

"We knew each other well enough to…"

"I'm aware of what we did," she snapped. "You could have told me who you were." She stood and stomped toward the tunnel. So much for her Zen moment alone.

"I introduced myself in all the ways that mattered in that particular circumstance." He jogged a couple of steps to match her pace. "Alice, please stop."

"And what?" She stopped and glared at him. "Listen to some bullshit you want to spin about the fact that you have someone back home who is waiting for you? Let me guess, she doesn't understand you… you weren't right for one another… you are taking a break…"

"Broken up in fact," he stated with a smirk. "Over a year ago."

"And your brother has no idea? I find that hard to believe."

"My brother and I are complicated. Alice, please stop and listen." He caught up to her again on the other side of the tunnel and closer to the street. She was angry and hurt but was still with it enough to realize that he hadn't placed a finger on her to prevent her from walking. Her ex had always been grabby, it was one of the things she hated about their relationship. Brent was respecting her; she would hear him out. Alice faced him, arms crossed, and attitude showing.

"I'm listening."

Brent dipped his head down, more to hide a smile from her than to gather his thoughts. She agreed that the entire situation was ridiculous, but she wanted to be the one to make light of it. When he did it, it was just irritating.

"I broke up with my fiancé, Nadia, a long time ago. It was mutual and amicable, we are still friends in fact."

"Peachy."

"Is that sarcasm?" Brent laughed. "Her boyfriend and I play cards once a month. He uses the money he wins from me to pay for the house he is building. They are getting married in the spring."

"Oh." Alice didn't sense he was being dishonest, but she had been lied to before. "So why does your brother think you are still engaged?"

Brent shrugged. "The long answer is something to explain on another day. It's complicated. The short is that I was embarrassed to tell him the truth."

"Fair enough." Her anger level dropped down another notch and she was starting to feel the cool night air. She wasn't nearly as worked up as she had been. The calming effect he had on her was registered once more, like the intimate moments they had shared less than 24 hours ago. "It makes sense, honestly. I stayed in a relationship longer than I should have so that I wouldn't be single, even knowing full well he was seeing someone else."

"So, whose ass am I kicking?"

Alice laughed. "No one we need to worry about. While our breakup wasn't amicable or mutual, he moved on."

"So, no card playing?"

"Not when we were together, but last I heard he moved to Vegas and is dating a Blackjack dealer, so maybe he likes them now."

"His loss is my gain."

"Is it? How would you know?"

Brent smiled and shifted his weight. "Do I really need to answer that?"

Swallowing her smile and shooting him a raised eyebrow, she decided her ego needed a response. "You absolutely do."

He took a step forward, close enough she could feel his radiant heat, but keeping his hands to his side. She glanced down. His fingers were flexing like Mr. Darcy's in the movie *Pride and Prejudice.* There was nothing hotter in her mind. Tipping her head up she looked into his eyes, the attraction making its presence known to every nerve in her body.

"I know now, like I knew last night, that one taste of you would never be enough. That the moment of sheer joy I feel every time you are in my arms, will only be worth it if the pattern can be repeated any time I choose it."

Her response came out in a whisper. "And would you? Choose it?"

"If I had a choice, yes. If it were Fate and I didn't, yes. If I had to rearrange the stars to make it work, 100%. I think we owe it to ourselves to see where this leads."

"What if it doesn't work out? I can't bear the thought of disappointing Tasha. And you have unresolved stuff with your brother. This has disaster written all over it."

"I'll talk to my brother; the conversation is long overdue. In the meantime, please consider seeing me again. You are all I have thought about since we met, and I want to learn more about you. Get to know you. Hold you in my arms and never let go."

He had moved closer, and she welcomed the warmth, her voice still filled with hesitation. "And if one day you do?"

"Let go?"

She nodded and whispered. "Yes."

"Not possible," he said with conviction. "But if that unlikely scenario were to happen, I promise you we will always be able to play cards." The response made her smile. It was the best indicator of who he was as a person, and how he treated the ones he loved. He took off his jacket and slid it over her shoulders. "You have to be freezing, let's head back. We can talk about this later."

"Before we go, I have one favor to ask."

"Anything."

"Kiss me."

6
BRENT

Brent had already been in town a few nights, and he still hadn't told his brother he was single again. On top of being a sub-standard Alpha, he was starting a relationship with the best friend of his brother's future wife, who hadn't been completely honest about her identity. It made sense that Sam hadn't told Alice he was a werewolf, but for Tasha to be best friends with her and not mention the fact that she was older than the buildings in New York City, was something he was curious about. He was also picking up on something with Alice that he couldn't quite put his finger on. Whatever it was, it was otherworldly, and she was unaware.

If he were being honest, he was being selfish. He wanted what Sam had, and Alice in a lot of ways represented that for him. It was like all the stars aligned when he met her. Like a cosmic shift occurred and clicked into place, creating an awareness of her that spread into all his senses. He could feel her even now as she started her day, unaware that he had imprinted on her without the need to mark her. Although one would argue the scratches on her backside were enough to make suitors scurry. They were quickly healed with a few laps of his tongue as they made love in her apartment after the rehearsal.

Hesitant to leave her warm side, he made it back to Sam's apartment by 3 AM. He had just finished his first cup of coffee when Sam came out dressed in his jeans and a button-up with a suit over his shoulders. He had brewed it to mask her scent, along with the change in his, but was afraid the strong brew wouldn't be enough.

"New blend of coffee? Why are you up so early? We don't need to be there until this afternoon."

"Couldn't sleep. Thought we could talk." There, the cat was out of the bag so to speak. There was no turning back.

"Sounds good." He hung his suit bag near the front door next to Brent's. There were just a few more things they needed to pack before they left for the venue. "What's on your mind?" He poured a cup of coffee, adding a splash of cream before sitting at the table across from Brent.

"I wanted to talk to you about the pack."

"Is everything okay?"

"Not really. I tried Sam, but I just can't do it."

Sam stood up and paced the floor. He could smell the irritation his brother was struggling to keep hidden. "Brent, I thought this was what you wanted? When we came back last year to get things back on track, you were happy with Nadia. What happened to the plans you had? Where is she really?"

"Zander is what happened. She is with him now."

"Zander? Dude, you lost your woman to Zander? I mean he's nice and all, but he isn't… well, you. What about your mating bond?"

"We didn't have one."

"What? But you said…"

"Listen Sam, I know what I said, but I lied to you. You have built a life here, and then found the one woman in the universe that is meant for you. I didn't want to ruin your chances at happiness."

"So, you were willing to forgo yours? That's fucked up. What about your happiness, Brent? I thought you were good there. It's the only reason I felt okay leaving."

"You knew deep down I was never going to find happiness by following the path you were meant for. I'm not Alpha material and leaving me with the responsibility because your heart wasn't in it was a bullshit move. We both know it."

"My heart wasn't in it because of all the things I saved you from when you were younger. We both know it's the reason I write what I do.

I needed hope, redemption, love, a fresh start. I found it here."

"You found it but sacrificed my future by doing so. I wasn't asked if this was what I wanted, I was told. I made the best of a bad situation."

"And lied about finding a mate. Made me believe I could leave it behind?"

Brent nodded his head. "I did. Because I knew that if I didn't you would come back, and I love you too much to watch you suffer through living someone else's life. You have more reason than me to turn your back on the responsibility. But I shouldn't have to live someone else's life either. I thought I could, man, but things have changed. I've changed. I'm not sure I can do it anymore."

"I'm not single anymore though. I'm building a life here with Tasha," Sam said with a sigh. "I can't ask her to go back there, it isn't safe for her. The only thing keeping her safe is that no one knows the truth about her here."

"I know. But I deserve to build a life wherever it suits me as well."

"Agreed. You do." He let out a breath and shook his head with re-signed agreement. "I haven't been fair. You were always happy in Wisteria. I hoped you would find contentment in settling down."

"I just haven't met the right person up until now, but I'm still hopeful."

"Me too. There is nothing more powerful than finding your match. I wish you everything I have with Tasha and more."

"Thanks, man," Brent said. He pulled his brother in for a hug, then took his chance. "Listen, I've been talking to Logan quite a bit over the last year. He's in the same situation in that Sera needs to be in Arizona more with the baby coming and Annabelle in school. I think we've come up with a solution that will suit all our needs."

"Go on."

7
ALICE

lice felt as though the truth of her heart was tattooed on her face. The looks Tasha had been giving her all morning weren't hard to decipher. She knew something was up, but didn't have time to unpack it. Alice knew how she felt, Brent was leaving in a couple of days and then she would have things to unpack as well. She didn't even want to think about the three card pull she had done this morning with her tarot deck. Something was about to be revealed, and Alice did everything she could to prepare herself for whatever came her way.

With her scent chamber freshened, and her Moonstone and Amethyst jewelry in place, she was prepared for her day. Until Brent was in the same room, that is. Then it was as if the oxygen was removed from the space in a single breath. His presence was a weighted blanket and a cup of cocoa with her favorite book one minute, then a jump from an airplane the next. The roller-coaster of emotions was unlike anything she had ever had with anyone else, and she wasn't sure what to do with herself. Running to Central Park today to ground wasn't an option.

A knock on the door and a call out heralded his arrival since he was acting as messenger between the couple. His deep baritone asked Tasha questions Alice's lust-filled mind couldn't decipher. Alice lifted her scent chamber to her nose and breathed in her stress-relief blend of lavender, geranium, lemon, and sandalwood. The oils calmed her nerves until he gave a covert wink which was when she realized that sandalwood was probably not the best scent to keep in the mix. She should have used a different recipe for the day. The flutters in her stomach started anew. He had just left when Tasha's voice startled her out of her thoughts.

"Is something wrong? You seem out of it today,"

Alice startled and spun around. "I'm fine," she squeaked. "Just getting nervous, you know how I hate crowds."

Tasha narrowed her eyes, then the questioning look was gone. "I know how you feel." She spun around and pointed between her shoulder blades. "Can you get the top few for me, please?"

"Of course." Alice went to her then fastened the pearl buttons on the beaded sheath Tasha wore. It was a beautiful shade of eggshell and the appliques and beading resembled jasmine blooms which was her signature scent. Since the choice was hers, Alice had found a bridesmaid dress with lavender blooms embroidered along the bottom edge to compliment. "You look beautiful, Tasha. I'm so happy for you both."

"Thank you. You are gorgeous today as well and I'm pretty sure there are those who would agree without hesitation."

Alice swallowed the lump in her throat. She wasn't ready for the conversation. "I have no idea what you mean, but thanks for the compliment."

Tasha took her by the shoulders and looked into her eyes. "I think you know exactly who I mean, Alice. His breath catches every time he sees you."

The kind look in her friend's eyes made her emotional. With tears welling, she smiled in relief at the friend who she could finally tell her secret to. She had figured it out on her own, thank the goddess. "I didn't know how to tell you. Brent and I just…"

A curt knock and crack of the door came before a call out by the photographer who made his way into the room. He introduced himself as Jacob and was a nice-looking guy, although younger than Alice would have thought a professional to be. Tasha had hired him because he worked alone and would be less of a distraction for the day.

He set Tasha up, then took his time moving Alice into place. His hand was warm on her lower back as he pulled her over an inch in one direction, then two in the other. His hand slipping to the top of her butt wasn't anything that bothered her, necessarily, but when it slid down past the globe of her ass and she looked up, she definitely picked up what he was laying down. He gave her an apologetic smirk and wondered how much of a turn on it gave him that she decided against the lines of the thong and was completely nude under her satin dress.

She would bet the amethyst she was wearing that he would ask for her number before the night was through. The fact that she had no desire to give it to him, or anyone at any point soon, spoke volumes. Brent had her rethinking things in that department. The first few clicks of Jacob's camera sounded, then came another knock and the squeak of the door hinge. This time there was no warning called out and nothing could have prepared Alice for what came next.

Brent filled the doorway, stepped in, then snapped it closed behind him. Somehow, he seemed larger to her, perhaps from the breaths he was taking in and out as if he had just finished a five-mile run. Thankfully the photographer was distracted with posing her and snapping his shots, so he missed the red glow of Brents eyes beaded in on his back. Tasha took one look at him, shook her head, and tipped her head toward the restroom. Alice watched him lumber toward the small room to the right, his eyes burning into hers and squeezing her heart until it hurt. Emotions radiated from him… jealousy, frustration, betrayal. Not necessarily directed at her, but she felt each one as if they were her own.

"He will be okay," Tasha murmured to Alice, then addressed the photographer. "Just a couple more, Jacob, then we can excuse my Maid of Honor."

Jacob nodded, busy with his work and apparently oblivious to the thick tension in the room. Alice could hardly breathe. She glanced at Tasha who was smiling at the camera but whose eyes reflected worry for a situation she didn't fully understand. Or did she? There was a knowing between them, but it was shrouded with a veil of mystery. It was like Alice almost had all the pieces to a puzzle she was just beginning to form. She smiled for a few more pictures, then excused herself before rushing to the restroom where Brent stood waiting, hands on the sink in front of the mirror and head lowered as if in defeat.

She came up behind him using the mirror as a shield between them, not wanting to look him directly in the eyes. Finally finding her voice, she whispered to him. "What are you?"

His voice, gravely, guttural, gave her chills she couldn't pinpoint. "A shifter," he said simply. He looked up meeting her eyes in the mirror. They were still red, but much less crazed. As if he had reigned them in but was still having a hard time controlling them. She looked down to his hands and the change had begun there as well. Clawlike nails and hairy knuckles replaced the well-manicured hands that had soothed her during lovemaking.

"Werewolf," she whispered.

"Yes," he nodded. "Alice, I have so much I need…"

She interrupted him, her hand held up and eyes closed. "I don't want to hear another word right now," she said quietly. When she looked back up, he had turned to face her, and his eyes and hands were back to normal. Or was it even normal? "I take that back. Your brother?"

"Also a shifter. Alpha in fact, although he left me in charge of the pack when he moved here."

Her quiet voice cracked on the next question. "And Tasha?"

He took a breath, unwilling to respond, then shook his head. "That is her business to share with…"

"What the hell is she?" Her voice snapped like a rubber band in a small space. She was on her last nerve. She didn't care at this point who could hear her outside.

"It's her place to tell you more. She's an Elf."

She turned away and nodded, proud of herself for taking in an unbelievable amount of craziness and digesting it like a champ. He took a step toward her, the warmth of his electric touch on her shoulder was immediately shrugged off. "Don't touch me, please."

He stepped back. "Of course," he said woundedly. "Alice I'm sorry. I knew I needed to tell you, but I was asked not to. It was explained that it was for your protection."

There was a knock at the door, then Tasha's worried voice from the other side. "Everything okay in there?"

Alice looked into Brent's eyes and whispered. "We will talk about this later," before responding to Tasha's question. "Everything is fine, we are coming out now." After taking a deep breath and pasting on a smile, she opened the door and walked out, leaving Brent in the bathroom alone. She had a wedding to get through, and then she was going home.

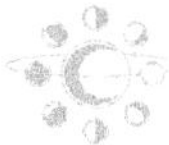

The ceremony was beautiful even with the friction between friends and lovers. They were all on edge, no one knowing the full truth of what was causing the turmoil, but all feeling its effects. Alice kept looking at her friend, the one she thought she knew so well and tried to see signs of Elf-like behavior. Did she know what an elf acted like? Were the books she always read any indication of how things really were? If Sam's books were based on his actual experiences as a shifter, who was to say that some of the Romantasy Books she loved so much weren't writing as own voices as well? Crazy to think that the fictional stories could be true, but here she was watching living proof there were mystical and magickal beings alive and well…and getting married.

Her anxiety was through the roof, and it took every bit of energy she had to get through the ceremony and pictures. By dinner she had a crippling headache, and she was ready to make her excuses. The wedding party believed they knew why she was leaving, but headache or anxiety, she couldn't handle one more minute pretending she was friends with people she didn't really know. Well…wolves and elves. Was this really happening? No one argued against her reasons, Tasha especially knew better since Alice's headaches were typically debilitating and quickly turned to migraines. She looked worried, but Alice gave her a small smile and told her she would text her later. The plan was to get some space, then deal with the aftermath later.

Her phone buzzed the entire way home. Text after text. Most were from Tasha, some from an unknown number. When she entered her apartment and locked herself in, she turned it off without reading the messages. What she needed right now was a hot bath and some soothing music. There was no way she was reading; she had had enough Fantasy for one night.

As soon as she locked and bolted her door, the shoes came off as did her gown on the way to the bathroom. She asked her device to turn on the lights as she made her way up the hallway and turned the water as hot as she could bear to fill her tub. A few drops of essential oil wouldn't be enough to pull the negativity, so she went back into the kitchen to slice some lemons, spying the roses Brent had gotten her the day before. She took a little too much pleasure pulling the petals from them Morticia style and dropping them in the bowl with the fruit slices.

"Sweet with the sour," she muttered to herself, marching naked to the bathroom and tossing them into the tub. She went back to the kitchen and made herself tea to wash down some of her prescription meds before carrying her mug back to the tub.

She needed some space to spread out all she knew and mix it with all that she learned. It was her process, one that had her rearranging and piecing together situations in order to know what to salvage and what to throw away. The thought that her friendship could be collateral damage made her stomach cramp.

After lighting several candles, placing the soothing tea on her bamboo tray next to her glasses, and turning off the bathroom light, she settled into the tub and laid her head back on the cushion she kept there. She was no more than a few minutes and a deep sigh into her soak when a sultry female voice had her snapping her eyes open.

8

ALICE

A whoosh sounded in the small space she lounged in. It was coupled with her awareness that there was someone else in the room. She slipped on her glasses. "How did you…"

The woman waved her hand as if dismissing her. As Alice tried to scream, she realized her body and voice were locked in place. Why not? She thought to herself. If werewolves were real, certainly witches could be. This one wasn't messing around.

"I need your undivided attention," the woman said. Her eyes were strange, as if gold were swirling inside like glitter in resin. "I apologize for keeping you restrained against your will, I typically ask for consent, but we just don't have the time, darling." She sat on the toilet lid and crossed her legs, looking more like a model in a photo shoot than a random woman sitting on a porcelain stool. "I'm Zilla, by the way, and I know what you would say is nice to meet you, so we'll just pretend you did. Okay with you? Perfect."

The last word fluttered from her tongue and rumbled in her throat, much like the purr of the strays that hung out in front of her store. As she watched her mannerisms, she realized those were cat-like as well and would have spit if she were able when Zilla gave her a confirming wink as if she were on the right track. If werewolves were real, why stop there?

"I have some things to say, and I am going to give you your voice back so you can ask questions. But the second you start screaming I'll take it away from you. Agreed? If so, blink twice."

Alice blinked, if for no other reason than she needed answers. Maybe this woman had some.

"All right then. Arms too." She waved her fingers, her long lacquered nails catching the light from the nearby candle.

Alice cleared her throat and took a sip of tea in order to harness the calm she didn't feel in the slightest. "Zilla, you say?"

The woman nodded and Alice sipped. "Why exactly are you here?"

"I'm here to help you," Zilla said. "It seems that my world and those who are in it are being thrust upon you and you're going to have some decisions to make. With you being a bookstore owner and all, I know you will understand and appreciate backstory. I'm here to give that to you."

As one never to skip a prologue, epilogue or author notes, she was intrigued. "Go on."

"Brent and his brother Sam come from a parallel world called Wisteria. It's where magick lives and creatures from all veils of the universe dwell. Sam was next in line for the position of alpha but after a disagreement with his father, then his untimely death, it was almost impossible for Sam to stay. He decided to follow his dream of becoming a writer, which eventually brought him to New York. Ultimately that left Brent in charge of being the alpha, albeit reluctantly, but Sam doesn't know that."

"What is this have to do with me?"

"It seems that Brent has set his sights on you and, more importantly, the universe has woven your paths. Where Fate dabbles, I assist, which is why I'm here. Divine purpose, and all that. Anyway, love match aside, you've also been practicing witchcraft and I'm here to tell you if you choose the life that Brent offers you, my sisters and I will fully support and train you. We need more magick makers in our realm and you have great potential as a sorceress. You aren't doing your power justice here."

"Even if all of that is true, I have a life here. Friends."

"A best friend, Tasha, right? Who is also from our world."

Alice didn't realize her mouth had hung open until she started her next sentence and her mouth was dry. Sip. Another sip. "Am I the only one in New York that didn't know she wasn't human?" What the ever loving…

"Human enough," she shrugged and checked an imaginary chip on her nails. "She's an elf, but we like her anyway." Zilla laughed at her own joke, waving her hand for effect. "Just kidding. Sam is crazy about her, and we love who he loves. For reasons, I will allow her to explain, she left a long time ago with no intention of ever coming back. So, now more than ever, Sam will hesitate to perform the duties he was born to. This put Brent in a situation that he's been trying to find a solution for. You just complicated things for him."

The irritation came out in an eruption and the water was getting cold. Alice couldn't help but be snarky. "Just get to the point. You're talking in riddles."

"You haven't seen riddles until you have met Fate, by the way. No one does them better than my sister. But you're right and I'm running out of time. To be blunt, our identities were kept from you for your safety and for the safety of the people you love who are living in a place that don't understand their kind. Many of us have lived in the shadows to survive, Sam and Tasha have chosen to live in the light. To do so they must keep pieces of who they really are hidden away. It's not the lifestyle I would choose, of course, because who wouldn't want to see all this and know me completely," she laughed, her eyes twinkling without the gold.

"Modest much?" Alice shook her head and put her mug down.

"I can see why he likes you," Zilla smiled. "Sassy. You will fit in just fine. Now, I must be going, and you may want to get dressed. Because in about 90 seconds he's going to be here and if you don't answer the door, he will knock it down. Your bond only allows him to read your thoughts once you consent to it and open the channel, but he can definitely pick up on your emotions. My guess is that he is on his way now to determine what kind of threat you are dealing with."

Zilla rose from her seat and checked her lipstick in the nearby mirror before finishing her thought. "Let him know I said hello when he gets here and Alice, give him a chance. I know shifters aren't easy to live with, but they are loyal and will move earth and shift time to ensure your happiness. You can ask me how I know if we ever see each other again and I hope we do. Remember what I said about your powers."

She snapped, releasing the hold she had on Alice's legs, then shrank down into a small black form, wearing an emerald collar. The shift confirmed what she had already known. As Alice pulled herself from the tub, the cat slowly faded. The last thing to disappear was her smile, not unlike the Cheshire Cat in Alice in Wonderland. Ironic.

There was barely enough time to throw on her robe before she had to respond to the pounding on her apartment door.

"Alice, open up. It's me, Brent." His voice was strained. Worried. Gruff.

She opened the door, leaving the chain in place and peeked out through the crack between the door and the jam. He had left his jacket at the venue, presumably, as she didn't see it anywhere. His hair was disheveled, fangs piercing his lower lip, and when she glanced down to his hands, what she saw there had her shaking her head.

"Nope. Not letting you in. You need to calm down."

"Who's in there?" He growled, which had her tipping her head and crossing her arms. She raised one eyebrow.

"Excuse me? This is my apartment."

He took a deep breath as if to center himself, then started again. This time his voice was calm and even.

"I'm sorry you're right. I'm just making sure you're okay."

"Considering you are almost the entire reason I am here right now behind a locked door, your statement is pretty humorous."

"You have nothing to fear from me."

"Yeah well, so far I haven't seen or heard a valid reason why that would be the case."

Brent shifted on his feet and scratched the back of his neck. "I know Alice I'm really sorry I came here to explain. Can you please let me in?"

Alice pointed her finger through the chained door crack waving it up and down at him. "You are not coming in this apartment until you calm all this down," she said with a gusto she didn't feel. "You can let me know when you're ready." She shut the door in his bewildered face and locked it, knowing full well, he could break it down if he really wanted to.

She sat on the couch and watched the shadows on the other side of the crack pace back-and-forth in the space outside her doorway. Her nerves were firing, her stomach in cramps, but for the first time in a relationship she was empowered. It felt good standing up for herself.

As she waited for Brent's decision, she thought about the romance novels Sam had written. The way the shifters in those stories treated their women, mates. If even a small percentage of what he wrote was true, Alice knew she'd be given anything she could ask for. That she would live out her life with undying devotion from a man who would do absolutely anything for her. He would burn the world down if she asked, not that she would. The instant attraction and obsession and connection made sense now as crazy as all of it was.

She had read enough about it to know what came next. And the fact that he was still here pacing the floor outside her apartment door gave her a thrill. Maybe this was her chance at living the fairytale. The question she had to ask herself next…was she ready for it?

9
BRENT

He paced outside the door until his nails were normal and the dark hair on the back of his hands had disappeared. A quick flick of his tongue across his teeth confirmed he was in control. He took a breath and tapped on the door, careful not to pound even though he was frantic to get inside.

"Alice?" He cleared the last of the roughness from his voice with a cough. "Can I come in?"

Her beautiful face peeked through the crack with the chain in place. She was less anxious now that he was calmer, and relief lowered his shoulders as she undid the chain and swung open the door. He had reset his approach; she would hear him out.

"Come on in. Have a seat. Can I get you anything? I'm going to have a glass of wine."

"Wine sounds amazing, thank you." He took that she was inviting him in and offering him a drink as a good sign.

She opened a bottle of Chardonnay and poured two hefty doses, walking one over and handing it to him before sitting across from him in her upholstered chair. She perched herself there as if she was royalty receiving her visitors. Her demeanor screamed no bullshit, a message he was receiving loud and clear.

He cleared his throat mainly to hide his bemusement. She would keep him on his toes. He was very much looking forward to it. "How's your headache?"

Alice took a sip of her wine and nodded. "It's better. Had I stayed, I'm sure it could've turned into something much worse. Probably shouldn't drink this, but not sure I can get through our chat without it, so wine it is." Not snippy, merely the facts. She was right, her staying would have been disastrous. Not only would she have learned more than she was ready for about their world, she would have also seen him get his ass handed to him by an elf. Not his proudest moment.

Sensing something, or someone, he sniffed the air, then put his nose near the top of his wine glass before taking a sip. "You're here alone then?"

Alice hid a feminine smile behind her glass. Guess he wasn't as nonchalant as he thought he was. "Yes, Brent, I'm alone. Although I did have a visitor. She asked me to say hello then shifted into a black cat before turning into mist and disappearing."

Brent closed his eyes and covered his mouth, rubbing his hand down his face. Fuck me. Alice was enjoying his discomfort and grinned as she took another sip of wine. "You know her then? She said you did. I was wondering how well since she's quite beautiful." No jealousy laced her tone, but he could sense a twinge. She was way better at nonchalant.

He shook his head. "There is nothing like that between us. All shifters know better. Besides, she's with Erebos and it's best to stay out of that relationship." He attempted to keep the fear from his voice, but Zilla and her sisters had a direct impact on his future. On anyone's they chose to mess with, honestly. "What did she have to say?"

"That you would be here and then I'd have a decision to make. Both things I knew already. What I didn't know was that my best friend, the man she was marrying, and his brother were all from a land that parallels ours and is filled with mystical creatures that I've only ever read about." She took a sip of her wine to soothe her shrill voice. Maybe she wasn't as collected as she led on.

"You're right, I should've told you. More importantly Tasha should've told you, but it's her history to tell. So, I'll tell you mine if you'll hear it now."

"I've got all night and have just opened a full bottle of wine, so I'm all yours. But won't you be missed at the wedding?"

He shook his head. "Sam and Tasha told me to come after you. No one's going to miss the Best Man, especially when my better half has already left the building."

Alice flushed at the reference, but didn't comment on it. She took a sip and waited for him to continue.

"Sam is older and was born into the alpha position, trained for it his entire life as a matter of fact. I never paid much attention to what needed to be done or what the pack's expectations were because I knew he'd always be there for us. But things happened that caused him to turn his back on that life and he chose to reinvent himself here, in New York. I suppose the romance genre was appealing because it's a genre of hope. I think he needed that at the time. He's been through some crap. Our father wasn't a good person."

Alice sipped her drink and was processing what he was saying. He liked that about her, how she quietly took in all the information before she made her thoughts known.

"Long story short, he abdicated his duties. I've been in charge ever since, but it doesn't come naturally to me. Once he met Tasha, and knowing a little bit about her history, it became clear that he wouldn't be back. I knew I would have to find a solution on my own for these duties that I only do out of obligation and love for my brother. He deserves to be happy, but so do I. And up until now, I didn't know how that would look for me. But after meeting you…I get it." He put the glass down on the table, elbows on the tops of his knees and bowed his head. The position always helped him ground. After a deep breath, he raised his head and looked into her jewel-like eyes. Her thoughtful expression radiated love and understanding. It made him weak, but at the same time gave him the strength to put his heart in her hands.

"Happiness for me is a woman with her nose in a book and her hand around a scotch on the rocks. It's the tingling feeling in my chest I get each time she laughs. It's the fact that she's the first thought in my head when I wake and the last person on my mind before I fall asleep. And it's the hope that she will allow me to spend the rest of my life, fulfilling her every desire. Happiness for me is the woman I'm looking at right now, Alice. Please tell me I still have a chance at having her in my life."

Tears were silently streaming down her face, but she composed herself with another sip of wine. He did the same as the lump in his throat from the emotions she was sending his way were almost too hard to bear. He wanted to take her in his arms, but it had to be something she asked for.

"I've made a life here, Brent, and if your responsibility is to your pack in another world. How do we make this work?"

He had his answer with her question, and a wave of relief moved through him and washed away his fear. From the look on her face, she could feel it too. He had his foot in the door and they both knew it. Thank the Gods. As she paid more attention to the feelings in her body, he started to catch pieces of the thoughts that were circling her mind. She wondered about the connection. If she decided not to pursue a relationship with him, would it still remain?

He nodded, answering her unspoken question, then moved to the side of her chair and held his hands out waiting for her to accept them. When she did, he lifted them immediately to his lips and placed a tender kiss on the inside of each of her wrists. He didn't want to pressure her to stay because of her soulmate status. She didn't need to know how it would break him if she decided to leave. He would focus on what he could offer her if she stayed.

"There is another Alpha in my world, Logan, who's in a similar situation. His wife, Sera, is from Arizona and they're back-and-forth all the time. We've been sharing duties, combining our efforts and it seems to be working well. If we had one more person sharing those duties it would be easier for us all, which is what I talked to Sam about earlier. His hesitation is of course Tasha, but my hope is that he will agree to share the role. So, to answer your question, I'll be able to share your life with you in the place you are most comfortable. If you don't want to change your life, you don't have to. I'll to whatever it takes to be part of your world."

"And no more keeping secrets? Even those that you feel are necessary for my safety?"

"I promise." She knew the truth of his words; he felt it inside his soul. He had passed her test. "Before I make my decision, I want to see your home, meet your friends. I need to learn more about your world. I also want to meet Zilla's sisters, she mentioned they could help me with developing my craft."

That Zilla had taken interest in her as a witch was surprising. Perhaps she was a better fit for his world than he had first realized. "She and her sisters are powerful. Their knowledge, endless. If you're sure…"

"I'm not sure about anything, frankly," she snapped. A quick breath and a sip calmed her next phrase. "But I do feel as if I'm missing a large part of who I am and that their offer might very well be the thing that brings me closer to my purpose. I do have a life here, but this also feels right to me. The choice is hard."

"Sera has a similar situation, so might be able to help guide you. She harnesses the element of fire. But please know if you decide that life isn't for you, I'm just as happy making our home here."

"Or both."

"Both works," he smiled. "Give me the word and I'll make it happen. The sisters have been around a long time and if Zilla has offered to mentor you, I think it is worth looking into."

"I would like that. I feel as though I have a lot to learn, and she seems like she genuinely wants to help."

"She has her moments," he responded diplomatically. He didn't say more, Alice needed to make her own decisions about his world and her role in it. That she was considering it at all took the pressure off.

Their clasped hands dropped to her lap, and she lifted one up to soothe the stubble on his face. It was the one thing that remained from his "wolf mode." He caught flickering thoughts of it rubbing across her stomach, then her thighs, which physically warmed her and quickened her breath. His little minx was frisky. She closed her eyes and then he heard her sweet voice in his mind. *I want this… you. Touch me, Brent.*

"Tell me where to start, my sweet." The connection she had initiated would only grow stronger with their bond. His hands were already soothing up her thighs and opening the robe as she sent him images of what she wanted. It was the coolest fucking thing he had ever experienced, and he was so thankful he had finally found her. Now he understood what he had been waiting for. Who he had been waiting

for. His mate. His life.

The growl rumbled from his throat as his voice responded in her mind. *"Anything. Everything. If the things I've heard about a mate connection are true, we are in for an amazing night."*

"Show me what you've got, lover."

He pulled her toward the front of the chair then slid his hands up to her breasts gently pushing her back into a reclining position. He laughed, and she tried to wiggle, locked in place by his arms, pinching her nipples. He lowered his head and feasted, sending images of what they would do next to her mind.

"Is this what you were thinking?"

10

ALICE

Tasha had the door to her store unlocked when Alice arrived. Knowing she didn't open for an hour and to have their conversation without interruption, Alice locked the door behind her and stepped into the calming space. Tasha already had scented candles burning and Alice caught the smoky scent of freshly burned sage. Her friend greeted her with a hug and mineral water.

"Thanks for coming so early. I figured we would both be busy today with last minute holiday shoppers."

"Fingers crossed," Alice smiled. They sat in the lobby in the over-stuffed chairs Tasha had there for weary shoppers. They were used most by the friends after hours.

"I wanted to apologize to you, Alice. For not sharing more about who I was, or where I came from. It made sense in the beginning, but not so much after we became so close."

"It's been hard to wrap my head around to be honest," Alice said truthfully. "I have pieced a few things together from past conversations and the small bits I learned from Brent and some crazy cat lady who paid me a visit…"

"Zilla?"

Alice nodded. "Yeah. She was something. Anyway, I thought if we were going to continue forward as friends, it would be best if we started fresh."

"I'd like that," Tasha's relief made her tear up as well. "So not sure what you've been told, but I'm an elf."

"I got that bit," Alice laughed. The ice had officially been broken and they were back to the easy friendship they had both come to value.

"Okay, well a little less known is that I'm over 500 years old and was born into royalty."

"Mother Goddess," Alice exclaimed. "I'd ask your secret, but I'm guessing it's genetics."

Tasha laughed. "Yeah, we tend to stick around. Anyway, my father is a purest and extremely traditional, so had lined me up for marriage at a very early age to Aldar, a prince from a neighboring kingdom."

"I understand now why you don't like reading Romantasys. A little close to home?"

"Exactly. And a little outlandish if you ask me, not realistic like what Sam writes." Alice watched Tasha's face light up at the mention of her new husband's name and wondered if she would look that beautiful when she spoke about Brent in the future. "I stayed much longer than I should have, but I didn't know any better. I thought Aldar being controlling was because he wanted to keep me safe. Once the abuse started, I realized my mistake. It wasn't until a Jinni came into my life that I started to see a way out."

"The Jinni helped you? Like granting wishes?" The story was getting more unbelievable as it unraveled, and Alice now understood why her friend hadn't confided in her. She would have never believed her.

"Yes. He was attached to a ring Aldar had given me, but he had no clue of its real power. The Jinni showed me a life beyond what I knew, worlds to explore, and ultimately arranged for my escape. In exchange, I agreed to take his ring with me and keep it far away from Wisteria."

"Where is he now? Do you still have the ring?"

Tasha shook her head. "The ring was lost to time years ago, and ultimately traveled back to Wisteria through various hands and circumstances. I've always felt horrible for letting him down, especially after all he did for me, but know now that Destiny wouldn't have had it any other way. The man I traveled here with was human and died not long after we settled here. I had to leave quickly after he did since I was no longer safe. Witch trials," she said as a way of explaining. "I've been traveling around ever since, and the ring ended up in an antiquities shop which is where Zilla eventually found it, as I've come to learn."

"I've met Zilla, and it sounds like I'll be meeting Sevilla also. The third sister is…"

"Fate," Tasha answered. "I don't know them well, but understand they are extremely knowledgeable, but also unpredictable."

Alice nodded. "If Zilla is any indication, I can see that. She did offer to help me develop my powers, though. Thinks I have potential."

"I do too," Tasha said sincerely. "You have a natural gift for spells and potions, they can help teach you so much more than I can. I'm excited to hear about what they have in store for you. So, are you and Brent doing okay?"

"We're better, but still working a few things out. He mentioned he had talked to Sam about the possibility of helping out in Wisteria, is that something you're on board with? Where is Aldar now?"

"He's in Wisteria, and Sam has warned him if he comes anywhere near me there will be hell to pay." Smiling at the thought, Tasha leaned back in her chair. "That was when we first met and, well, you know the rest of our story. It's nice not being alone anymore, and for someone to have my back. I'm hoping the same for you."

"It's been offered," Alice said. "We will be making a trip there to see if I like it."

"I think you will, they have built a wonderful community there. Zilla had us go back to meet with Sera and Logan early on in our relationship, but when we got there the conflict, she was worried about, had been resolved. Now I realize some of it had to do with Brent and Nadia's break up which was kept from us. By the way, you will love Sera, she's great."

Tasha stood up and went behind her counter, bringing back a purple bag filled with tissue and handing it to Alice. "You left so quickly from the reception I didn't have a chance to give this to you."

Alice accepted the gift with a smile. "Thanks, Tasha." She pulled the frame from the bag and looked into the smiling faces of two baby business owners cutting a red ribbon in front of Roots. "We were so young," Alice said with awe, then caught herself. "I mean I was."

Tasha laughed as Alice stood for the hug she had waiting for her. "I was young in my experience of being a shop owner," she said with chagrin. "I guess that is something."

"It is something," Alice agreed. "And it is something that we are now moving into a new phase of our life, and still doing it together."

"Growing roots."

"That will stand the test of time. Thank you for trusting me with your secret, I'll keep it safe."

"I know you will."

She gave Tasha another quick hug then gathered her backpack. "I'd better be going. We need to open in five. Thank you so much for the gift, I love it."

"Let me know how you do today."

Alice left through the front door with a wave and her step was much lighter as she made her way to her store. A quick flick of her lights and placing cash in her register was all she needed to do to ready herself for the day. The buzz of her phone and the glance at the screen brought an immediate smile to her face. She thought about her wish to have what Tasha had with Sam, and realized she had found the person who lit her fire and she was definitely ready for her happily-ever-after.

Good morning, Beautiful. Have any plans for lunch?

Not yet. What do you have in mind?

You. Always you.

EPILOGUE

The two brothers worked out a schedule with Logan to alternate months of the year. They shared the Alpha duties, which worked easily around his wife Sera's due date and their daughter Annabelle's school schedule. Since she was going to college in Arizona, they were back and forth regularly, so for the first few months Logan got the lighter load. Alice spent the first month after the busy holiday season building up her online presence and limiting her in-person store hours by hiring some staff.

Brent and Sam spend a lot of time there initially with the other couples building community housing in order to consolidate the packs into one central location. Because the elements split their time between the earth realm and Wisteria, they decided to build homes there as well. Brooke, Tara, and Amie, worked with Sera to set up magical barriers surrounding the complex to keep unwanted visitors out, which gave Tasha peace of mind when she spent time there.

The first thing Zilla and her sisters taught Alice was how to create a portal between her world and theirs, allowing her to travel easily between the two. This allowed her to feel comfortable leaving part-time staff to cover for her when she wasn't there, knowing she could get back quickly if she needed to.

Learning to harness her newfound abilities was exciting and she was an apt pupil. In the months she and Brent had been traveling back and forth, she had perfected some of the easier spells like speaking to wildlife or growing a plant. What no one had realized until it happened one day, was that Alice had the ability to shift into small animals. Brent said he wasn't surprised that the first animal she turned into was the very pet name he used for her. Minx.

With Zilla teaching her how to navigate her shifting abilities, Sevilla teaching her alchemy, and Fate teaching her the art of divination, Alice was well on her way to becoming a powerful sorceress. Brent wasn't surprised by that either, since he insisted, he had been bewitched since the day he met her.

He was in the kitchen of their home in Wisteria pouring two glasses of wine when Alice walked through the door carrying a large bag of carry-out food from their favorite Thai Restaurant.

"Sorry I'm late, there was a line at Thai Garden," she said. The bag was set on the table before she launched herself in his arms to land the kiss they had both been talking about for the past hour. Their bond had grown stronger, and they were getting good at the long-distance conversations, even on either side of the portals they used to travel between worlds.

"That made up for it," Brent smiled. "That and the fact that you have my favorite scent on."

"You like it? It's something new I've been working on."

"Makes me want to eat more than Thai food." she had no control over her body when he spoke to her in that tone. His deep voice blanketed her very senses.

"We can arrange that," she cooed.

He handed her a wine glass, then took her other hand and pulled her toward the spare room. "Hold that thought. I want to show you something first."

"I like the sound of that," Alice giggled as he tugged her to the closed door and pulled a lavender sash from the doorknob. "Oh, what do we have here?"

Laughing, he shook his head and tsked. "You have a naughty little mind tonight." He held the tie up pointing to her eyes. "I have something to show you, may I?"

Excitedly she agreed, then helped him tie the fabric over her eyes pulling it in place. "I love surprises!"

"Ready?"

She nodded and he took her hand and opened the door, leading her through to the center of the room then giving her instructions to stay in place. The complete trust she was showing wasn't lost on him, they had really come a long way in the past few months. When he was in place, he instructed her to remove the sash. The look on her face registered confusion at first, then surprise, and when she saw him kneeling in front of the display he had worked on all afternoon holding a black velvet box in his hands, her eyes started to well.

"Oh, Brent."

"Let me get this out, my love."

She nodded then covered her mouth with her hand in an attempt to stop the tears. It didn't work.

"You've changed your life to be in mine and I wanted you to know how much I appreciate and love you for that. I wanted to give you a space in my world that felt like yours, a special place of your own. You are everything I could ever want in a partner. Please say you will spend the rest of your life with me." He opened the box to show the amethyst and diamond ring inside and rose to his feet when she stepped forward, her head nodding and tears streaming down her face.

"Yes. Oh honey, it's gorgeous," She threw herself into his arms and squeezed as if her life depended on it. Then pulled back and took another look at the ring before looking once more to the display behind her new fiancé. The entire wall was lined with new bookshelves and pockets of light, bringing attention to the favorite things she had brought with her to make herself more at home. The picture of her and Tasha was there, along with a recent one of her and Brent in a matching frame. There were candles and crystals from Tasha's shop, as well as books that looked as old as time.

As she rubbed her hand along the spines, she realized some of them were books she had been studying from at Sevilla's house. "When did you have the time? Where did all the books come from?"

"The guys all came over and we busted it out right after you left for work. The books are donations from the sisters and some of the members of the community, they are all yours to keep. I also had Tasha bring some from your place since she knows what you like to read."

"Thank you, Brent. This is unexpected and amazing."

"So are you, Alice. Since the day we met you have humbled me at every turn. I love you."

"I love you, too."

"Now where did that sash go? I have some plans for that comfy looking chair in the corner."

"Ah, there's my little minx."

To Brittany C

Thank you for beta reading
everything I write and for your
kind words of support when I am
feeling low. I am so fortunate
to have you on my street team
and love that you have my same
wacky sense of humor. Long live
Statler and Waldorf!

the
JINNI'S WISH

*Each older than time itself...
they have both been searching
for someone to trust.*

Desperate to find the source of his power before it falls
into enemy hands, a powerful Jinni must accept help from
a widow, whose caution might eclipse even his. Will they
discover that trust in each other is the biggest risk of all?

1

Sevilla's back started to pinch, so she straightened from her task. The potatoes weren't going to plant themselves, but she had been at it since sunrise and needed a break. Inside her stone cottage, her feet echoed mournfully in the spacious kitchen as she walked to the sink. As she washed the soil from her hands, she realized that the last time she had planted that particular variety of potato she had been happily married. That was no longer the case.

Her quaint cottage had always been a welcoming place, but the past few years had been rough on her. She found it easier to be outside, rather than in the house where so many memories came to roost. The house hadn't been the same since Ryker had passed ten years before. Each year seemed to get harder.

Not knowing how long she would be, she slipped her shawl from the hook near the door and tied the fabric around her slender hips. She often lost track of time on her walks and the added warmth it provided would be welcome once the sun set. Wrapping the cheese and sausage remaining from her breakfast in a cloth napkin, she loaded a small basket with the makings of a picnic. Her task took only moments; a picnic for one.

She crossed the room and opened the door, quick to close it on the past that haunted her. With a deep breath, she drew in the bird's light-hearted song and the babbling of the creek near her house and turned her back on her sorrow. It would be there waiting for her return. She would deal with it then. For now, she would walk.

The magical land where she lived had all manner of creatures, but for the most part each species kept to themselves. Most tolerated visitors, although Sevilla had run into some crabby Nymphs long ago that were clearly irritated by her female presence. They had been all coos and winks until they realized that she wouldn't offer her husband to them as a plaything. The hisses and glares came faster than a shifter changes shapes. That was the last time she went anywhere near the water during a full moon, since their memories were long, and she no longer had Ryker around to buffer their fury.

She turned from the path then walked deeper into the woods. Only then did she realize where her feet were leading her – to the place where her husband once worked his magick and connected to his element. That was long before Fate stirred the cauldron of destiny and changed their lives forever. It still hurt to think of the part her sisters played in her husband's death. She hadn't seen Fate or Zilla since he died, but she wasn't really sure she was ready to.

The walk would take longer than the hours remaining in the day to travel, so she created a magical opening between two large oak trees that lined her path. She'd been there so many times she could envision the place she wanted to travel with hardly a thought. The magick opened for her. Sparks spun around the outer edge of the entrance, allowing her to pass through to the Woods of the Winds, where the element of Air was most prominent.

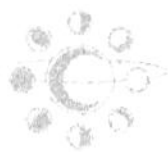

The stone altar was as she'd left it, albeit the neglect was evident by the weeds and debris that littered the path that led to it. It saddened her to see the space in such a state of disarray. Since it would be some time until the element of Air found an appropriate host, the area would remain in wait until a keeper of the energy came to claim it.

It also didn't help that the harpies had left their nests after the death of their Queen, since they were the ones that tended to the housekeeping of the sacred space during Ryker's time as the element. Zilla's boyfriend, Erebos, had a lot to answer for, killing Celaneo and leaving the harpies without a leader, but she wasn't sure she would ever get the answers she sought. The only thing she remembered from that terrible day was the way the light of their energy had woven around him before a powerful explosion knocked her unconscious.

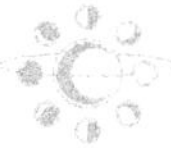

During her walk, the lack of sound struck her. Every bird had abandoned the site. It made her wonder where the creatures that related to an element would go while the powers were absent from their domains. Was there another area of Wisteria where the creatures gathered? Or perhaps they met in other dimensions, such as the Earth realm where her sister, Zilla, frequented. She hoped that wasn't the case. A few of the species were hard enough to control in the magical realm where she lived, so she couldn't imagine having humans witness some of their antics.

She recalled the disaster with the pixies, who played a starring role. It was the entire reason why the magical portals they traveled through were now reused. New portals hadn't been made in decades. In Sevilla's opinion, no more would appear until the new hosts of the elemental power managed them.

Once she reached the altar, she traced the triangular symbol with the line through it that was carved on the top side. There was dirt in the grooves of the etching, and she bent down to look on the underside of the table where Ryker used to keep his brush. It was still hanging from a metal stake that had been hammered into the rugged black marble. As her love had done countless times before, she used it to brush the layers of dried mud from the table surface. Her memories were speaking so loudly that she was startled by the voice and snapping of twigs behind her.

"Are you the new host for the element then?"

Sevilla jolted and spun, wielding the brush in front of her like a weapon. "Is it your habit to sneak up on people?" Her tone surprised him, based on the widening of his expressive brown eyes, but was quickly replaced by interest and a smirk.

"Had I intended on sneaking up on you," his voice lowered as he stepped closer, "you wouldn't have heard me at all."

"The twigs gave me warning," Sevilla said with a smile. This man was not threatening, but he had powers. She could sense fingers of energy reaching across to her and testing her. He was gauging her ability as well.

Another step closer. "They were stepped on for your benefit." Again, with the grin. Not only was the man handsome, but he was sure of himself. His powers were nowhere close to the same level as hers, but like her, he was an immortal. Or at least came off as one. He held out his hand. "I'm Kadar."

She took his hand in hers, noticing the calluses and the strength in his fingers. She tried to get a feel for his magical heritage through the firm grip of his handshake but came back woefully short. "Sevilla."

His energy zapped her nerve endings, and she quickly pulled her hand back from the shock. He wasn't anything dark like a Vampire, but he definitely was someone who knew his way around both sides of magick.

"Nice to meet you," he said with a quick bow. It was more of a nod and less like the formal greetings she had witnessed in the fairy court. He hadn't fully formed his own magical path, but perhaps he was an assistant to a Mage or other magical creature. She wondered if Theo knew him. As the elf king, he knew all manner of magical beings.

Sevilla felt her cheeks warm at his perusal. His ebony hair and stubble, along with the dark clothes he wore, gave her the impression of someone who could blend into the night. But his eyes were what had her pulse racing. Their mocha color, streaked with hints of gold, reminded her of the Tiger's eye pendant she was given when she was little. She hadn't worn it in years, but if she were to pull it out of the jewelry box where it was kept, she was sure it would match his eyes perfectly.

He tipped his head quizzically, and she lowered her gaze. She had stared a bit too long. He cleared his throat and asked his original question. "So, are you the element of Air then? The keeper of this realm?"

Sevilla shook her head. "I am not." She cleared her throat against the sadness that threatened to choke her. "I do keep these areas clear for those who will arrive in the future though."

He nodded as though he understood. "I generally steer clear of these areas unless I know that they aren't being used. Those who are meant for them tend to be possessive."

"They can be," Sevilla agreed. She turned back to the stone table and finished brushing off the dirt as she spoke. "But you really can't blame them. It is a great responsibility to keep the magick safe and out of the hands of those who would abuse it."

"Well said," he said quietly. Kadar came around the other side of the altar, so he was in her line of sight and bent to pull at some of the weeds that had sprouted around the base. Soon, they were working in unison to clear the area, the companionable silence soothing.

The stone table was set to rights quickly and Sevilla took a step back to admire their handiwork. "Thank you for your help, Kadar. It means more to me than you can know."

"You're most welcome." He handed her a piece of fabric, pulled from the inside of his cape. She glanced down at it and hesitated. "It's clean," he said, giving her a wink.

She took the offered fabric and wiped her hands. "Thank you," she said quietly. She did the best on her hands as she could with the fabric, deciding that on the way back she would find some water to wash them in. She was curious about him, especially since the elemental areas were located in the most remote parts of the land. The altar where they stood was in the eastern-most portion of Wisteria and was edged by a mountain range that spanned for miles. It was not somewhere a creature could get to easily.

"You aren't from this area," he said conversationally. She had started to walk toward the clearing she and Ryker used to picnic in, and Kadar was following. She didn't mind. If she was being completely honest, it was nice to finally have someone to talk to. Her sisters didn't dare visit, and the fairies and sprites that lived near her house spoke in exhausting circles. She hadn't been in the mood for their hijinks, so had been keeping to herself.

"No, I live on the opposite side of Wisteria. More toward the west."

"So closer to water's domain?"

Sevilla nodded. "Yes, that's right. Just north of that." He was more familiar with the elements and their areas than was comfortable. What was he? While she still wasn't necessarily feeling threatened, she found herself more and more curious about the magick he wielded.

Kadar's hand took hold of her elbow, as she stumbled over a log she hadn't noticed in the path. He kept it there until she found her feet again and then slid it away as if nothing had happened.

"You are a long way from home," he said thoughtfully. "Is this area so important to you then?"

All the areas were equally important to her, although at one time, this was one of her favorite places to be. She was tired of being lonely and decided to be honest. "I believe in balance, so I cater to each of the four elements equally. I am ashamed to admit that I neglected this area as it was hard for me to face it."

"Why is that?"

She stopped, and he paused his steps as well. He looked at her, his eyes squinted and his head cocked. He was the first man interested to hear what she had to say since Ryker had died and the words struggled to cross her lips. Conflicting emotions churned within her, as he waited for the words she choked on. With a sigh, she finally voiced her thought. "It was my husband's realm."

"Was?"

Sevilla looked in his eyes, tears coming into her own when his expression softened. Her voice cracked as she responded. "He passed."

His hand reached for hers, and she allowed the comfort he offered. There came the opposing feelings again: trust then concern, acceptance then fear, attraction then guilt. His fingers were strong and soothing, and she was lulled by the patterns he was caressing with his thumbs. Yes, the last set of emotions was giving her issue. That his response was sincere made it all the harder.

"I'm so sorry to hear that." He gave a slight squeeze, then let her hand fall to her side.

She responded the only way she could without crying. "So am I."

2.

Sevilla quickly soothed the awkward moment by walking to a fallen tree and opening her basket. It was one of the places she and Ryker had searched for mushrooms and wild asparagus. She decided it was better to honor his memory than to wallow in her loss. The guilt she felt was new and clearly brought on by the simple attentions of a handsome man. Kadar was still with her and seemingly had nowhere to be, so she invited him to lunch. She wanted to learn more about him. The tightly coiled power he held intrigued her.

"I brought the makings of a picnic. Would you care to join me?"

His expression confused her. His eyes registered surprise and the smile that widened was truly joyous. If she didn't know any better, she would have thought that she had just given him the stars. It was a ridiculous thought since they had only just met, but it made her happy, nonetheless.

"I would be honored to share your meal. You are so kind to ask." He bowed with one hand, palm up, and the other bent behind his back. The gesture was quick, but formal, and confirmed her suspicions that Kadar was familiar with the niceties of court.

"It is nothing fancy," she replied. "And it will be lovely to have some company. Could you help spread the blanket?"

"Certainly." He took the woolen fabric from her hands and snapped it out over the moss near their feet. The fabric floated down over the soft surface, making a comfortable place to sit.

Sevilla placed the bundles of meats, cheeses and fruit on the blanket, and they sat on either side of the spread. She had brought some wine as well and was pleased when he nodded in response to her offer of a glass. She never liked to drink alone, as it was a reminder of her solitude. Raising her glass, she made a toast.

"May our memories soothe us, the universe provide for us, and new friendships find us."

He clinked his glass to hers and raised it. "Well said. I'll drink to that."

The wine was spicy, one of the last bottles her sister Zilla had brought back from the Earth realm. Sevilla still couldn't bring herself to talk to her, but she would miss having her wine in the evening if she didn't. It made her wonder if she could figure out how Zilla was traveling and do it herself. She didn't frequent the Earth realm but perhaps it was time.

He was examining her again; his eyes didn't miss a thing. He was either extremely perceptive, or her body language was easy to read. She packed up her melancholy thoughts and munched on some cheese. As intended, Kadar took it as a cue to take some food as well.

"So, Kadar, do you live around here? I thought I knew most of the people in the area, but we haven't met before."

"No, we haven't," he said quietly. His body was still relaxed, but she noticed his fingers tense slightly around his wine glass. He took another quick sip and cleared his throat. "And I'm not from around here. Not exactly."

It was information he was nervous to give, but perhaps he felt the same about her as she did about him. There was a curiosity that seemed to go both ways as well as a guarded trust. His response confused her.

"Not sure what that means, unless you live here some of the time?"

"It's hard to explain," he said, shaking his head. When he looked up, sadness in his eyes begged her to help him navigate his pain. Perhaps they had more in common than she knew.

"I'm a good listener and might understand better than you realize. Try me."

He paused with a breath, then started his explanation. "You seem familiar with magick." He waited for her nod and then continued. "And no offense, but it seems you may be older than you look."

Sevilla couldn't help but smile. This man had manners. Never discussing a woman's age had been a hard and fast rule since the dawn of time. He had a very nice way of saying she was much older than him, and she found herself immediately forgiving his transgressions. He was right. She was much older than pretty much anyone for that matter. "None taken. And you would be correct." She wasn't getting into her immortality and the purpose for it. She still didn't know anything about him, except that he was perceptive. This friendship, if there was to be one, would need trust—something she didn't give away freely.

His smile radiated from him, and his body relaxed. She wasn't sure why, but she sensed that he was about to share something about himself that very few knew. "I'm older than I look as well," he said quietly. He glanced over his shoulder behind him and leaned over slightly. She leaned in to listen, waiting for the secret he was now trusting her with. "And I'm familiar with your magick, as well as my own."

Sevilla was confused. "But there is only one universal magick," she said. "It embraces us all and is what must be maintained and balanced or there is chaos."

He smiled and shook his head. "Your universe supplies the magick for your world but there are others."

"Worlds or Universes?"

"Both."

Sevilla had so many questions. He looked serious, like he truly believed what he was saying. She wondered how she could dispute his comments, even if it contradicted what she had believed her entire existence. The universe worked in mysterious ways, and who was she to question its abilities. Wisteria and the Earth realm were connected by the magick through use of portals. It wasn't such a stretch to think there might be a connection between other worlds as well. There was a lot to consider.

"I'm assuming you have abilities." She waited for his nod and then continued. "These abilities aren't tied to the magick I'm familiar with?"

"I don't believe–," he broke off mid-sentence at the snap of a twig and disappeared in a puff of blue smoke. Sevilla was shocked, looking around her to see where he might have gone. Vanished. The smoke that indicated his presence had all but disappeared. Another snap caused her to call out.

"Who's there?"

A sultry voice came up from behind her and startled her. "It's me, Villy."

Honestly, the last person she wanted to see right now. By the time she entered the clearing, the blue smoke from Kadar was gone. "Zilla, you startled me."

"I can see that." She looked at the blanket and the half-filled wineglass that Kadar had left behind. With a raised brow, she glanced at Sevilla's glass then sauntered over to the place he had just been. "You have company?"

Sevilla had every right to embrace the feeling of distrust that came over her. She decided to keep Kadar's presence secret for the time being. Something was telling her that Zilla didn't need to know her business, and she still wasn't sure who, or what, he was.

"No," Sevilla shrugged, as she poured more wine in each of the glasses. "It's ridiculous really. I pour one for Ryker and then drink them both."

Zilla's eyes softened, and her curiosity was redirected. She took the glass Sevilla offered and sat next to her, in the very spot Kadar had just been. There was no sign of him. Zilla raised her glass for a toast, with tears of guilt brimming in her eyes. Sevilla wasn't ready to forgive her for her part in Ryker's death, but she was her sister. She would eventually have to, she supposed.

"To Ryker," Zilla said softly.

"To my love," Sevilla answered, as Zilla lowered her eyes and sipped her wine. There were so many questions she had, especially since she hadn't witnessed all that had transpired when Ryker died, but her emotions were still raw at the sight of her sister. "Why are you here, Zilla?"

Her sister looked up, and her face reflected pain that, in a terrible way, made Sevilla feel better. At least she was showing remorse. After a deep breath, Zilla answered her sister's question. "I want to come home."

Sevilla noted Zilla's shaking voice but gave no power to it. "Well, no one is stopping you," she answered with a snap. "Just the ghost of my dead husband."

Zilla's eyes widened, and she placed the glass down after draining it. She stood up looking down at Sevilla, the depths of her sorrow etched on her beautiful face. The sisters were two of three mirror images, each of the two differing only in outward emotion. Zilla's demeanor wreaked with sorrow while Sevilla's churned with rage. They couldn't know what their third sister, Fate, felt, as she hadn't been in contact since the night they killed Ryker.

"I can see this was a bad idea," Zilla said quietly. "Your pain is still fresh."

"How can it be anything but? Not only was my husband taken from me, but I wake only to hear that it was my sisters who hold the blame. I lost my entire family in a flash."

Zilla looked over her shoulder and to either side of her before responding. "I can explain," she whispered softly. She took a step toward her, and Sevilla held up her palm to stay her.

"I don't want you to explain. I just want you to go," Sevilla said firmly. It was the first time she had ever spoken like that to her sister. If she knew Zilla, it wouldn't be the last.

Her sister lowered her head and nodded in acceptance. Shoulders drooping, her voice found its way to Sevilla's ears as she turned and walked into the treeline toward the altar. "I love you, Villy. Ask Fate about the part I played and then we'll talk." She raised her hand and waved with a wiggle of her fingers without looking back, which was one of Zilla's signature moves. In and out of your life just long enough to create havoc then leave before witnessing the result of her meddlings. Good riddance.

Sevilla closed her eyes and took four deep breaths, calling upon each of the elements to grant her patience. By the time the last breath was drawn, Zilla's presence could no longer be detected. It made her curious to know which portal Zilla had used. Sevilla resigned herself to check them all on the way back home. Her sister was entirely to blame for the Pixie incident, one of many things she could pin on her sister's nonchalance.

Sevilla packed the picnic back into her basket and was getting ready to walk back to the altar when a chilled breeze surrounded her. It tickled her skin, causing the tiny hairs on her arms to rise. If she wasn't mistaken, someone or something, was watching her.

"Kadar? Is that you?"

The response was silence, but the presence was still in wait. Sevilla reached out, scanning the area with the fingers of her mind but with no results. If the hair on her arms hadn't told her otherwise, she would have thought the area was clear. It was time to go. The visit had been draining, and she worried her powers weren't working as they should be.

She walked past the stone altar, taking one last look at it before moving up the path that led from the clearing. It would be some time before she would feel strong enough to come to this place again.

As she closed the portal behind her and continued to make her way home, the focus of her mind touched on the man she had met. She couldn't help but be curious about him and wondered what had made him leave their conversation so suddenly. It had to have been Zilla's impromptu visit, although Sevilla knew that there was a possibility she would never know. That didn't sit well with her. There were too many questions about Kadar that needed to be solved. The most important of which was, what was he?

Sevilla had made it home without incident and spent the rest of the evening in front of the fire, reading from her book of shadows. She thought it was possible that it held clues as to what type of creature Kadar might be, or at the very least, eliminate what he wasn't.

3

Sevilla wasn't expecting company, but someone was coming none-theless. Her broom had fallen to the floor no less than 6 times this week alone. She had spent the days after her visit to Ryker's altar working in her garden and canning, both of which helped keep her mind occupied. Her nights had been spent researching the various creatures that frequented Wisteria. She wasn't able to shake Kadar from her mind, and her curiosity had already eliminated a large number of possibilities.

From what her instincts were telling her, she wouldn't be alone for long. Unable to get a sense of who, or what, was on its way, she prepared for her visitor. She wasn't used to getting them, as her house was placed in a remote part of Wisteria to deter them. While she did have the occasional creature wander into her domain unaware, it didn't happen often since her wards limited their ability to find her. In a strange way she was glad the stranger was making the effort to find her, it had been much too long since she had entertained guests.

After tidying a few things in the kitchen and removing her apron, she placed her basket of magical tools at the center of her table. Disguised as a centerpiece, the crystals, stones and herbs would be placed centrally if she needed to get to them. She slipped her hand in her pocket and palmed her favorite amethyst turning its smooth surface over in her hand and absorbing its calming qualities. The knock at the door came sooner than she had expected.

As she took the few steps needed to her door, she reached out with her energy and touched on the mystery on the other side of the oak panel. The magick was familiar but still as unknown as the day she had met him, even with all of her recent research. She opened the door to a smiling Kadar and was surprised at the nerves that made her stomach tremble. It was ridiculous really. She wasn't a young woman, but he made her feel like one. Alive. For the first time in years.

"I hope I'm not intruding," he said with a slight bow. "I came to apologize."

Sevilla waved him in. She had already discounted a number of magical creatures that he could be, so she felt safe in doing so. He definitely wasn't a Vampire or Succubus, which would be the least welcome creatures to her home. "So nice to see you again, Kadar. Please come in."

He stepped inside, and she closed the door behind him. He stayed just a few feet inside the threshold and was looking around. "You have a lovely home. Very welcoming."

"Thank you. Please have a seat here. I was just going to have some mulled wine, would you like some?"

"Smells delicious. Thank you, yes. Our time was cut short during our last conversation, which is what I came to apologize for."

"No apology needed," Sevilla said and placed a mug of a fragrant red in front of him. Still sore from digging potatoes, she hoped the extra cinnamon and cloves she added would do the trick. She took her place across from him, still well within reach of her tools, but she was almost entirely sure she wouldn't need them. "If I'm to be honest, you were probably better off."

His eyebrows pinched as did the corner of his eyes. "What makes you say that?"

She glanced up and gave a small smile. His curious tone covered a slight defensiveness. It made her want to soothe the worry from his face. Obviously, they were each worried about the impression they made on the other. Sevilla had no doubt they would be friends for some time.

"Right after you left, I had a visit from my sister."

"And that is a bad thing?" His head cocked, and he flashed a smile. His face was so expressive, she could watch it for hours. She found herself matching his grin.

"You don't know my sister."

His laugh rumbled across the kitchen and straight into her heart. Oh, how she had missed that sound. It was nice having a man in the house again. "You are right, I don't. She's hard to handle?"

She nodded her head and sipped with a smile. Their eyes met and shared a secret that neither would voice. Knowing they had a kinship on some level was enough for now. "She can be a bit much."

"Well, it was still rude of me to leave as I did. I'm sorry."

"Apology accepted but completely unnecessary," she answered. The awkward pause caused them both to take sips of their wine. It was the same for Sevilla each time she met someone new. She lived a solitary life for the most part and relationships didn't come easy. She had an idea.

"So, how are you at chess? I've grown weary of playing alone."

"I know enough to make it an interesting game."

"Wonderful. Follow me and bring your cup."

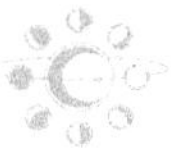

They settled in the den adjacent to her kitchen. It was separated by a fireplace that opened in both rooms, and the fire she had built earlier in the morning was keeping out the afternoon chill. She wasn't willing to cut down the trees that shaded her home, so when the sun dropped below the horizon, she just put another log on the fire.

"I'll do that," Kadar offered, taking the log from her hand and placing it in the opening. He stoked the fire and she situated herself near her chessboard. After the fire was burning brightly, Kadar sat in the seat across from her and looked down with curiosity at the dark piece of stone.

"My chessboard is a bit different," she explained. "It lights from the inside. You'll find your pieces in the small drawer in front of you."

While Kadar pulled his pieces out and lined them to the side of the board, Sevilla waved her hand over the top and sent a surge of energy toward the smooth surface. The board formed between the glowing squares of light and shadow.

"This is amazing," Kadar exclaimed. "The detail on the pieces is incredible. Is this Zeus?"

It was pleasing to her that he knew his Greek Gods. "It is. The pieces are representative of the Olympians, however, it surely can't represent them all."

Kadar waggled the king piece before placing it on the board. "Especially, with all the trouble this one can get into," he laughed. "You have female pieces. Hera doesn't look happy."

Sevilla laughed. "Well, I can't imagine she is. I will warn you now that her eyes will follow him wherever he is placed on the board. He is never far from her sight."

"I can imagine that is true. So, the pieces are magical as well as the board?"

She nodded. "Yes. I had it made some time ago by a craftsman in Greece. He had an extra special talent for creating things infused with magick."

The final piece he placed was the rook, a tiny version of the mountain the Gods lived on. "His attention to detail is incredible."

"He was a gifted artist," Sevilla agreed. "None of his pieces have made it through time on the Earth realm, which is a shame. I believe I may have the last of what he created."

"A treasure to be sure. Any special rules?"

"No, the game is played traditionally. Just know that sometimes the pieces will take matters into their own hands once you make a move."

"So, these ones with weapons?"

Sevilla grinned. "Let's just say you want to pull your fingers back if they start to wiggle."

Delight crossed his face, and Sevilla was relieved to see his boyish charm. It meant he was more relaxed. He rubbed his hands together and gave her a wink. "I believe the first move is yours."

Sevilla made her move then sat back. She watched him touch a piece without moving it, then after a moment, transfer his fingers to another and commit to his move. Once his decision was made, his move was decisive. She couldn't help but compare him to her late husband. Ryker had also played that way. After a few moves, Kadar noticed her watching him, and his curiosity got the better of him.

"Is everything alright? You seem pensive."

Sevilla shook off the past; it obviously wasn't a good look on her. She gave him a quick smile, one that wasn't forced which surprised her. "I'm good, just observing the competition."

"Oh? And what do you see?" His tone was the tiniest bit flirty, and his eyebrow raised to match the corner of this mouth—a mouth Sevilla was becoming obsessed with. A sip of wine allowed her to swallow what she wanted to say. The attraction was getting harder to ignore.

Her emotions were all over the place and were almost impossible to reign in. His grin deepened as he took a sip from his own mug, glancing down to her neck where she felt her pulse fluttering beneath her flushed skin. She had yet to respond to his question, but as he relaxed into his seat and leaned against the arm, it seemed to her that he had already received his answer.

Sevilla blinked. She had been staring and cleared her throat as she concentrated on her next move. If she wasn't mistaken, she heard a quiet chuckle which was quickly dowsed with another sip from his cup. Her answer moved softly across the chess board, and she was surprised to hear just the tiniest bit of sass coming from her lips.

"I see a man that is perhaps a little too sure of himself." She slid her knight to capture his pawn then pulled her hand back to watch the show. The tiny Satyr was no match for Artemis, who pulled back her bow and shot him through the heart. As his pawn disappeared, his face filled with delight.

"That was amazing! Where did the piece go?"

"They line themselves up in the drawer," Sevilla answered.

He immediately opened his drawer and glanced at the satyr securely placed in the velvet space designed for him. "Incredible. I've never seen anything like it."

"Nor will you," Sevilla said with pride. "The game has evolved over time, adapting to its environment much like we all have. While it started out special, time has only made it more so." It seemed that now it was his time to observe, and she took another sip to cool her cheeks. She pointed to his glass and shifted in her seat to rise. "Would you care for more wine?"

"Absolutely I would. Thank you."

Sevilla was glad for the small break in filling their mugs. She needed to regroup. It had been some time since she had entertained a handsome man in her home, and she was surprised to see that marriage to Ryker hadn't left her weaponless when it came to flirtation and her ability to channel it. While she wasn't nearly as good at it as her sister, Zilla, it was evident from Kadar's reactions that she must have remembered how to do it reasonably well.

If she was going to get involved with Kadar, which seemed entirely possible considering the signals they were each sending, she needed to get some answers first. It wasn't that she cared what he was, as she had many lovers over the centuries that came from various cultures and magical abilities. She just wanted to know what she was getting into.

He had a warm smile waiting for her when she returned to the room. He had shifted in his seat and secured a pillow from the nearby couch, propping it behind his back. She was glad he felt more comfortable with her. As she took her place across from him, he spoke.

"So, in the woods we were speaking of magick."

"That's right," she nodded. "And your theory that there is more than one universal source for it."

"Just so," he said with a smile. He seemed delighted with the fact that she had remembered. How could she not? She thought she knew everything, had lived through endless variations of what life could be, yet here was a man who was giving her a new world to explore. She had thought of nothing else since their meeting.

"I believe we were also discussing our particular abilities."

Kadar smiled and moved his next piece, capturing one of her nymphs with his bishop. His piece was represented by none other than the charismatic Hades, so after a fair amount of groping, the nymph went off willingly. It never surprised Sevilla when it happened, since she had known way too many nymphs in her time – they were a sensual lot. She glanced up into Kadar's smirking face, and they both laughed.

"That was quite the show," he said. "Not sure I want to open the drawer to see what they are doing."

"I wouldn't advise it," she laughed. She moved her bishop, a tiny version of Hecate, halfway up the board then leaned back into her chair. She glanced over to Kadar whose aura was glowing a bright blue, as he considered his next move. It was the same color as the smoke she had seen him morph into that day in the woods. While blue auras typically represented intuition, in his case, she felt it meant something more. "Kadar, I've been around a long time, but I've never met anyone like you."

He glanced up from his move, careful to keep his fingers on the rook he'd been considering. "In all honesty, that doesn't surprise me. Our kind tend to stay hidden from others."

"And why is that? It gets so lonely at times for me, but the choice was taken away from me. Why the chosen solitude?"

His features tensed, but he was not angry, only pained. His eyes told her a story of loss and hardship that she was sure she would hear over time. The smile that was meant to soothe her, only broke her heart. This was a man who had known little peace. He cleared his throat and shared his secret.

"I am of the D'Jinn and born into servitude. Solitude is the only thing that allows me to escape my fate."

Ч

Sevilla had prepared herself for any number of confessions from Kadar, but never had she considered he was a Jinni. Fear of his ability was overridden by fascination of finally meeting a creature of his caliber. She didn't know much about their culture but had heard the myths that tied their destinies to objects and wishes. Some cultures called them genies.

He was fidgeting, most likely regretting that he had confessed his truth. She covered his hand in hers and gave it a gentle squeeze, saying the one thing that she would want to hear in the same instance. "Your secret is safe with me, Kadar. Always."

It was the right thing to say. His shoulders fell away from his ears, and the breath he was holding came out of him in an audible rush. If relief was a substance, he'd have been covered in it. "Thank you, Sevilla. That truly means the world to me."

Their eyes locked, and a moment passed between them which entwined their fortunes and sealed their fate. His thumb paused from drawing soothing circles on the back of her hand. As he lifted her hand toward him, he turned it over palm side up, and she allowed him to pull as close as the chess board between them would allow. His face lowered, and he placed a gentle kiss on the center of her palm, his warm lips creating ripples of pleasure that radiated up her arm and into her heart. She closed her eyes to the feel of it, committing the act to memory. The feelings she registered confused appreciation with attraction, and she couldn't keep them separated.

As he raised his face from her palm, she opened her eyes and loosened her hand from his grip. She cupped his whiskered cheek, soothing the bristly hairs and gazing into his rich brown eyes. They reflected both the feelings she had registered but attraction was more prevalent now. She had never felt this way so quickly with anyone before, not even her late husband. It confused and thrilled her that Kadar felt it too.

Her voice quietly spoke her truth. "I know the weight of secrets and my essence is strong. Yours will not go beyond this place unless you will it to be so."

She lowered her hand and he sat back, visibly bracing himself to share his story. She had known a great many creatures over the centuries, some long dead who told tales of lives lived that she could hardly imagine. She had kept each and every one locked up safe in her memory. It was her nature, her purpose, to honor the past and to keep the stories safe for the future. She was curious to know how Kadar's past tied to hers.

"I was created, not born, and have been alive for more centuries than I care to remember. When I came into existence, my soul was tied to an object which can be used to summon me from wherever I am in the multiverse. The object and I are connected. One cannot survive without the other."

"And that object, where is it now?"

"Somewhere here in this land which is why I've come. To find it before someone else learns its secret."

"That it controls you," Sevilla whispered. Their eyes met, and he gave a quick nod, confirming her comment.

"Just so. I am obligated to serve the owner of the object until death or the completion of their wishes separate us. If I am unable to find the object before the next person knows it's worth, I know no rest."

"If you don't mind me asking, what is the object? You mentioned that you followed its call here?"

He nodded. "That's right. My last obligation was fulfilled, but I lost track of it in the realm I was kept. It was just by coincidence that I found my way here once more and felt its energy." Kadar paused and looked at Sevilla a moment as if to decide if she was truly worthy of his secret. He made his choice quickly and the next sentence came from him in a rush. "It's a ring, a sapphire, to be exact."

"A ring?" Sevilla considered just how impossible finding something that small could be in such a large land. "Does it just disappear and move on to the next place then?"

"Sometimes. Sometimes it is given to the next generation of the family who keep it but lose track of its true worth. In those cases, I have been able to secure it from auctions or pawn shops. There are also times it has a mind of its own and disappears entirely from the realm, only to show up in another."

"How can you possibly find something so small in the vast number of places that exist?" Sevilla couldn't wrap her head around the number of possibilities.

"It is a little easier than you think, since I am tied to the object. But I have to admit, sometimes it takes me a few decades to narrow down its location. By then, it is entirely possible for someone to find it and learn its secret."

"That it grants wishes?"

"That's right," he nodded. "Three to be precise. There are times that I am bound to a particular person for a lifetime, especially if they fear the outcome of the wish they desire."

"I can see where that happens," she mused. "The ramifications of a wish can be toxic, even deadly."

"I have found that to be so."

"Something must have happened to the last person who owned the ring. Is that why you are able to be here with me?"

"Yes. They passed away." He shifted in his seat, and his hands tightened around his glass. There was more on the subject that he wasn't going to share, and Sevilla sensed it had to do with the person who controlled him last. Not wanting him to be uncomfortable, she brought the conversation back to the ring.

"So, before you could find the ring, it was passed on?"

"That's correct."

"And which realm were you in when fulfilling your obligation?"

"The Earth realm. I've been there for some time to be honest, after being taken from this land long ago by someone I befriended. Through no fault of hers the ring found a new owner and was always passed on with the secret of its worth. I have been chained to that realm for what seems like eternity."

"What changed?"

"The last owner died without an heir or the completion of her last wish," Kadar said quietly. His face reflected sorrow but also love. The person who had controlled him was someone he had grown to care for. "I wasn't able to secure the ring before it was sold. After, it disappeared from the realm entirely."

Sevilla's mind started piecing together the parts of his story, with the knowledge she had of the Earth realm, and those who traveled back and forth between. "And when you followed its energy, where did it lead you?"

"It was odd at first, since the energy led me to a brick wall in an alleyway behind a tavern. It was only after I discovered the wall held an illusion-covered doorway that I realized it had traveled back here."

Her suspicions were confirmed. The ring had to be with someone that journeyed to the Earth realm from Wisteria. That would narrow their search. Especially, considering her sister had just come from there and was notoriously bad at closing and hiding the portals behind her.

"The doorway brought you to the area where I met you the other day?"

"That's right," he said cautiously. "You act as though a light has come on and illuminated your thoughts. Do you know of what I speak? Have ideas that could help me?" His excitement was increasing and was highly contagious.

She stood and paced the room, it was how she did her best thinking. So, who else besides Zilla was traveling between the realms? Could it be that Erebos was here also? Or Mila, the shifter they had taken to Earth to live when she needed to escape her family? Thinking back to how Erebos had met the Harpy Queen Cela, it was entirely possible that there were more creatures traveling there than she had realized.

"I haven't seen the ring, but I believe that there are only a small number of creatures that travel between here and Earth. At least that's my hope. If we can narrow down who has been traveling between the two lately, we might be able to find your ring."

He stood and took her hands in his. The smile on his face could hardly contain his excitement. "That is wonderful news. Where do we start?"

She worried her lip, and her eyes squinted as she tried to concentrate on the path they would need to follow. His excitement waned, as he anticipated the bit of reality she was about to share. The reality that would keep him from his goal, at least for now.

"That is where our trouble lies. Some of the people we need to talk to are the ones that I am avoiding."

His shoulders drooped, and he let out an exhale. "Your sister?"

"Precisely," she said with exasperation.

"Well, I am one step closer to finding it than I was a few days ago. I have scoured this land and haven't been able to narrow down its call. I have found hope now in your friendship. If you will help me, I promise to heed your advice. I have never had so much trouble narrowing my search in the past and have run out of options. Will you help me, Sevilla? Please."

As much as she didn't want to speak to her sister, or see Zilla's power-hungry boyfriend again, she couldn't tell this man no. Finding this ring would be the only way he would be able to regain his freedom, something she now realized she had always taken for granted. It was important to her, in a way she hardly understood, that she help him find his.

"Of course I will help you, Kadar. But we need to come up with a plan."

His embrace found her quickly, and her arms circled naturally around his waist, as her breaths took in the scent of him. He smelled like her garden after a rain, fresh and crisp with an undertone of the earth that she dug in each day. She drank him in as his face turned into the side of her head, and she felt his lips press there. His whisper tickled her ear. "Thank you."

"You're welcome," she whispered back. While the moment could have easily turned into something more, she gave it back with the intent it was given. As an offer of friendship.

He buried his face onto her shoulder, and his frame relaxed into the hug. A weight had been lifted from his soul and it felt natural to soothe his worries by rubbing his back. Tears of gratitude he could no longer hold back quietly dampened her shoulder, as they stood there holding each other in tender unity. Two broken souls had found one another, and for each of them, the moment was a turning point. There was trust given by one, while another let go of her past.

She gave him a moment to pull himself together and then gave him a final squeeze before breaking the embrace. He wiped his eyes and gave her a wink, as if to say his emotional outburst would be their little secret. Sevilla smiled back, indicating with a sweep of her hand that he should take his seat at the playing table. She walked to the kitchen to give him a moment to regroup and dropped the empty mugs in her sink. By the time she took her seat, he was settled and contemplating his next move.

"What's the plan, my lady?"

She smiled at his question. "I find that the answers come to me when I contemplate my next move. For now, we'll just play. In the morning, we will see the questions in a different light. I have a room you can stay in, since it will be late when we finish this game."

"You are a special find. I am really glad to have met you, Sevilla. Destiny bringing us together has been one of the highlights of my existence."

"I'm glad to have met you too, Kadar. We will find the answers for you, I promise."

He glanced up, and the adoration in his eyes was something she would strive to be worthy of moving forward. She wondered about destiny and about the designs that her sister Fate had put into place most recently. Could everything that happened, including Ryker's death, be part of some unknown path? Could Kadar be part of, not only her future, but all of theirs? As always, there were so many questions, and the answers would only be reflected in the past. So, until their actions became part of that narrative, they would have to be patient.

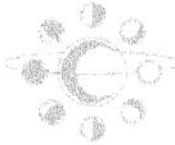

They had played well into the night, and Sevilla offered Kadar the room at the top of the stairs. It was the smallest room but the one that was in the best shape, as the others were in various stages of remodel. It saddened her to see he wasn't used to such comforts, as was obvious from the expression on his face. Especially, when he saw the modern amenities she had included in the adjacent bathroom. The sunken tub was one of her favorite places to relax.

She went downstairs and blew out the candles. Tidying for the morning, she realized she had forgotten to offer him some water and filled a pitcher from the hand pump in the sink.

When she knocked on his door, she got no answer and quietly called out his name. Still with no answer, she opened the door wide enough to call his name again and heard his rich baritone echoing from the bathroom. The glow from the lamps shone under the crack beneath the door, and she heard the splash of water as Kadar sunk into his bath.

She placed the pitcher of water and a clean glass onto the nightstand just inside the door next to the oil lamp that served as the sole source of light in the room. Smiling to herself, she listened to his beautiful voice singing a song that lightened her soul and wondered at the meaning of his words. The feeling it invoked was love and hope, and she was glad in her small way that she was able to provide it to him. Leaving him to his privacy, she quietly left the room before her imagination ran away with her.

5

The next morning, Sevilla had already plucked the ripe produce from the garden and was pulling a warm loaf of bread from the oven when Kadar joined her in the kitchen. The shadows under his eyes were gone. He looked rested. He was quick with a smile which pleased her; she had always been a morning person and it made her happy to see that he was too.

"Good morning. You're up early. Do you need any help?"

She shook her head and pointed to the table. "I'm up before the sun—old habits—and no, thank you. Have a seat and help yourself to some breakfast. I'll get this sliced. Do you need anything other than butter or honey for it?"

"No, both sound perfect. It's strange having someone cater to my wishes for once," he said with a grin.

A quick glance over to him showed the merriment in his eyes. She was glad to see his mood had turned. The lavender she had burned the night before had settled them both. She took her seat across from him at the table and passed him the plate of sliced bread.

"I thought about what we should do," she said. "We should check first with the people I know who frequently move between Wisteria and the Earth realm. Some of them may not be around, but it is a good place to start."

"And if they aren't around?"

"It will be easier for us to snoop."

Sevilla looked up to see his reaction to her suggestion that they might be doing some sneaking around. She was happy to see there was no judgement in the lines of his body. On the contrary, his boyish grin warmed her heart. His excitement was contagious.

"Are there many that travel to and from this realm?"

"I didn't think so but now I'm not so sure. There are a few we have placed on Earth for their safeguarding, especially if they have had trouble with their people. The shifters most commonly, but we have re-located a few elves as well. And my sisters and I have always had the ability to move freely between the realms."

"The sister that just visited? The one that interrupted our picnic?"

"That's right. Her house is one of the ones we will need to search, so I hope she returned to Earth with Erebos like she was told to."

"Erebos?"

Sevilla nodded. "Her boyfriend. He did some truly evil things. My sisters, in trying to re-balance his powers, caused my husband's death. Let's just say that none of them are welcome in my home for some time."

"I can understand why." He nodded. "I'm sorry for your pain, Sevilla. Losing someone you love at the hands of a person you trust is never easy."

He spoke as if he understood his comment to be true. It made her wonder about his past, and the instances that made him the man that she was now getting to know. The layers of the past built up like skin, sometimes thinned and bruised, most often thick like leather. The choices made often determined which you grew; she had learned that the hard way.

"I'm not sure I will ever be able to get past it."

His eyes softened, and his hand reached across the table prompting her to reach her fingers toward his. He gave her fingers a gentle squeeze. "Time has a way of softening the pain. We don't have to forget, but eventually we need to forgive for our own sanity."

She released his fingers and pulled her arm back, taking a bite of her bread to swallow the lump in her throat. "I'll get there, but so much of what happened was kept from my view. I was unconscious at the time and only after Fate told me what transpired could I piece it all together.

Neither of them has tried to contact me in over a decade. Until now."

"You are probably better off. You will need time."

"That is what I tell myself," she answered softly and quickly changed her thoughts to the order of the day. She busied herself with clearing the table and packing some of the food in a basket for their journey as Kadar ate. She wasn't sure what they'd run into or how long their searches would take, and a snack would be welcome if the day grew long.

Kadar rose from his seat and brought his plate, helping her with the dishes before taking the loaded basket from her hands. He waited by the door as she tidied then swept some ash over the smoldering logs in the fireplace. There wasn't anything nearby that could catch, and she hadn't lit any candles that morning, but the habit formed after the fire she had centuries before. The last thing she took was her shawl from the hook near the door and waited as Kadar opened the door and ushered her out. His attentiveness was a balm soothed over her loneliness.

The early morning mist had evaporated in the rising sun. They didn't need to walk far; the portal to Zilla's domain was just over the hill near Sevilla's house. Once there, Mila's cottage was within walking distance, since all the shifters lived in the same general area.

Kadar shifted the basket to his left arm and offered her his right. She slid her arm through the crook he made, glad for the warmth and stability it provided.

"I can create a portal just through these trees," Sevilla explained. "It won't take us long." She slowed her steps and slipped her arm from his. "Wait here. This will take but a moment."

Sevilla swept her arms wide in a circle, starting from above her head and sweeping down to her sides, before pushing out in front of her palms facing forward. The entire motion took less than a few seconds, and the doorway it opened would save them a two-day journey.

"That's just like the opening I found that brought me here," he remarked. "It's very similar to many portals that I've found between other lands as well."

"My sisters and I have used them often in the past but have closed the ones that were being abused by other creatures. Zilla has a terrible habit of leaving doorways open which, I believe, is how you were able to come here."

"I'm glad she is so absent-minded," he laughed, as he followed Sevilla through the portal.

She turned and clapped her hands together, sealing the opening shut behind them. "For once I am too," she answered. "Otherwise, we might never have met."

Her comment prompted a smile on his handsome face, which she was finding easier to return without feelings of guilt. She was a widow, not a married woman. Perhaps it was time to let go of the past. He was an interesting and charismatic person, one that she longed to know more about. She was ready to bring someone new into her life, especially since the alternative was the solitude and she had already tired of that.

Taking the path that led into the dense woods, Kadar took Sevilla's hand and navigated her over large stones and branches that crossed their path. Zilla liked her home located in the darkest and thickest part of the woods. As social as she was, she never cared much for visitors that didn't arrive on her terms. On that they could agree.

"Not that I mind the walk, but if you have magick at your disposal, why is it that you create the doorways so far away?"

"That was actually Zilla's doing," Sevilla said. "She was creating doorways any place she went and when she lost track of them, she made new ones. Half the doorways had never been closed and were being used freely by creatures who had found them. Some good and some not so good."

"That could be a problem. Especially, if they gained access to Earth or other realms."

"Precisely, so we made a pact. We closed almost all of the doors she had created and limited their openings to areas outside of our domains. That way, if something foul were to use it, they wouldn't pop right into our house.”

“Makes complete sense. And also allows for you to place wards around your homesteads, which I notice we are pushing through now.”

“She must have been here recently to renew them. Her house is just through this set of trees.”

“It looks simple and not what I imagined after being in your home. This looks more like the cabin of a huntsman.”

Sevilla looked at Zilla’s home with a critical eye. “I suppose it does, but don’t let the outside fool you. It is much larger than it seems.”

“So, another illusion?”

“Precisely.” They stepped up to the front door, and Sevilla knocked. “Zilla, if you’re here, open up.” There was no response, not even the footsteps of someone retreating into the house to avoid them. Sevilla reached out with her powers, trying to sense if there was any energy nearby, but the only one she could sense was Kadar.

She cracked open the door and peeked inside. The stale air from a house long closed tickled her nose. “Zilla?” Her voice echoed back to her. It was obvious no one had been there for some time. She must have placed the wards quickly from the outside and left like Sevilla had requested. At least she hoped that was the case, as it would make their search easier.

“We need to be quick. Although it seems no one has been here, I don’t want to get caught snooping around. Zilla isn’t the most pleasant person when you cross her.”

“It won’t take me long,” Kadar said. “I’ll just center myself over here and see what I can feel.”

“There is a lower level as well, so you may want to start there. The stairs are through that door.”

“I’ll be right back,” he said, as he puffed into blue smoke and disappeared beneath the oak door she had indicated. His ability to travel much quicker than they could wasn’t lost on her.

Sevilla went into Zilla’s sitting room. The room held far less furnishings than it had last time she was over, which if she was being honest, was years before. Had she taken some of her belongings over to the home Erebos had been creating for himself? That would make sense to her, since the house seemed so sparse. It was also entirely possible that she and Erebos were still in Wisteria, staying somewhere other than her place.

She scanned the magical tools on Zilla's mantle and was irritated to find that half the crystals were ones she had thought were misplaced. She picked them up and dropped them into her pocket, gasping when she came across the locket she had thought she had lost. "Why that little…"

"I don't think it's here," Kadar said, as he entered the room behind her. "Did you find something?"

"Only half of my belongings," Sevilla groused. "I even asked her if she had seen this. Unbelievable." She scooped the locket into her hand and dropped it into her pocket to join her stones. "I'll need to come back when I have more time to search. I'm sure this isn't all she has of mine."

Kadar waited for her to exit the room and then walked behind her, pulling the door shut as they left the house. Sevilla looked up at him, curious as to how he could have known so quickly that his ring wasn't there. He answered her unasked question after seeing her puzzled look.

"It calls to me," he said. "It's more of a feeling, a vibrating hum that rumbles in my chest, way less than a visual thing. The feeling starts up miles away, so in the case of her house, I knew we weren't even close."

"Mila's home is close by but if what you say is true, you would be feeling the hum by now."

"It won't hurt to try. We should exhaust all options. Besides, we might find something helpful to aid our quest."

Sevilla nodded. "True. Okay, follow me."

6

A few hours later, Kadar and Sevilla were sitting on a log deciding where they would search next. Mila's home had also been empty and had even less in it compared to Zilla's.

Sevilla explained that when they had relocated the young shifter, Mila, to the earth realm, she had made a home there and had never looked back. She had even married a human, although word had gotten back to Sevilla that he died during the explosion of Mt. Vesuvius in Italy where the couple lived. It had occurred at the same time she and her sisters had stripped Erebos of his powers in Wisteria. Even though the deaths happened in parallel worlds, Sevilla felt a certain kinship with the young widow since she had lost her husband at the same time.

They took time searching the area since Kadar hadn't been able to get through the wards that Zilla had placed around her domain earlier. He wanted to be sure not to miss anything. Sevilla explained that, because she had access to the area and he was with her, he was able to get through now. The sisters always allowed the others to pass through at will.

"And what of your spells? I was able to approach your home without any trouble."

"I changed them to allow you access. I hoped after we met, that you would search me out." Sevilla blushed. The words had come out much bolder than she originally intended. Now that they were voiced, she was relieved. She no longer had to hide her desires behind her sorrow.

Kadar looked pleased, a grin tickling his face, but not fully taking hold. He was trying to stay on topic, but he didn't allow the opportunity to pass. "I'm relieved you said that, since the alternative was going to be standing in the woods outside your home until you left for a walk."

The thought warmed her. As romantic as that sounded, it wouldn't be practical. There weren't many comfortable places to sleep and the pixies would have chased him away with their mischief. "There are times I don't leave the house for days."

"You're worth it. I would have waited."

Her breath caught, and his watchful gaze drank her in. He waited as a range of emotions fluttered through her awakening heart. By his reaction, he knew her response, but she needed to voice it aloud anyway. It would confirm to her mind, what her heart already knew.

"I would have liked that."

His smile beamed. There was no doubt that they would be addressing the subject of their relationship at a later time. There was too much chemistry to deny the opportunity they were both willing to explore. She had much to look forward to. Kadar was one of the most engaging people she had met in a long time. The fact that he was handsome as sin was a bonus.

He cleared his throat and took a sip of the water she had brought from home. She had been staring at him again. Lowering her eyes downward, she concentrated on their task and less on the attraction she could no longer deny. She mentally berated herself and tried to get her mind on track. Even after a full search of the area, they had come up empty-handed. Time to look elsewhere.

"So, your ring disappeared recently?" Sevilla passed Kadar another piece of cheese before biting into the next slice of sharp cheddar herself. The tang helped cool her earlier attentions.

Kadar turned slightly and shifted his legs. It seemed to Sevilla that he had been just as affected by their conversation as she had. It was good that they were changing the subject, now was not the time.

"That's right. It disappeared within the last few weeks."

"That eliminates Cela's house. She's been gone for a few years."

"Cela?"

"Celaneo, the Harpy Queen. Erebos killed her, which is what started this trouble in the first place."

"He is that powerful?"

Sevilla shook her head. "Not anymore. He was one of the elements. Erebos was gifted with the power of water. My husband, Ryker, was Air, Fate's boyfriend Anton was Fire, and our friend, Theo, was Earth. When Erebos decided he wanted more than the power he was given…"

"Things turned toxic."

"You could say that—more so imbalanced. Now what we are left with is the three sisters of destiny not speaking and the men in their lives killed or banished to the void. Erebos seems to have come out of it unscathed." She tried to curb her bitterness but it flavored her comments just the same.

"Even if it seems someone has gotten away with something, the Universe has a way of leveling things out. He won't continue to go unpunished."

"I know. It is just so hard to remain positive sometimes. How can I accept the terrible things that happen based on their Universal purpose, for a future I can't even fathom? My sister Fate has that gift—it's tangled her tongue now, so she can only speak in riddles. This is the first time in my life I have been truly upset with the duties the Universe has mantled us with."

"I understand better than anyone about the roles the Universe forces upon us," Kadar said quietly. Sevilla's guilt warmed her cheeks.

"Kadar, I am so sorry. What you have been through is unimaginable, and I am embarrassed to be wallowing in my own sorrows. It doesn't make for good company."

"You are wonderful company and my life has challenges, as does yours. I didn't want you to feel sorry for me, but my point is that sometimes the Universe has us go through some terrible things to prepare us for the next level of our journey. I believe that opening yourself up to the challenges that you face will make you strong enough to walk your next path."

She let his comment sink in and it soothed her soul. "You are one of the most enlightened people I have ever met."

"If I make it look easy, I suppose that's something. As you said, there are days it is hard to be positive."

"It seems we have a lot in common."

"We do indeed."

She allowed herself to bask under his careful attention for a moment and then got back to the task at hand. "So, if you're ready we will have time to check one last place."

"Lead the way."

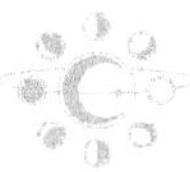

The area where Erebos lived was at the far end of Wisteria, surrounded only by the mountains from which he had fashioned his home. Sevilla had only ever been to it while it was being built and never while Erebos was present. Zilla had been excited to finally have a home that would offer her seclusion. After having so much of it over the past few years, Sevilla wondered why Zilla was so quick to embrace it.

The portal she created from Zilla's brought them to the outer edge of the domain. While she had originally been surprised that Erebos hadn't made his home closer to the water he had been connected to, she now understood why. He had never connected to his element as he should have and always hungered for more power in a way that was unnatural. Creating his home here would have allowed for him to practice his growing skills without knowledge of what he was doing, which was precisely what had happened.

"I seem to recall a side entrance that Zilla used here. A pathway that takes you up along the side of the mountain."

"I feel a slight pull from this direction." Kadar pointed left, which was the direction Sevilla had remembered the door to be. She had only been there a handful of times.

"That should be it. She has the opening hidden with an illusion, but it won't take us long to get through."

"You would be amazed just what kind of places I can get into." Kadar smirked, and Sevilla couldn't help but laugh.

"I can only imagine. And I think that you being in your alternate form will be the best way to search their home."

"I can also be invisible," he said, as he disappeared. She could only tell where he was by the location of his voice.

"I'm not able to sense you," Sevilla said, as she reached out to touch him. "Simply amazing."

"I am here beside you but behind a veil," he explained. "Because I am in an alternate dimension, you are unable to detect me with your magick. It isn't the most pleasant place to be. There are all manner of D'Jinn who have access to the same place but for temporary use it comes in handy."

He popped back into existence on the other side of her and offered his hand. The pathway they were traveling was a bit rocky.

"I can see that. Would you be able to speak to me in that form? Directly I mean, but without sound?"

Kadar stopped walking, and she turned to face him. Her innocent question had brought seriousness to his face. He placed both hands on her upper arms, as if to brace her for what he was about to share.

"I could connect our thoughts. Why do you ask?"

She realized now that maybe he was right. Perhaps not all magick was created equally. Was the magick he tapped into more powerful? Different? She was excited to learn of its possibilities.

His eyes reflected concern, and any playfulness had long left them. Sevilla warmed under his touch. After she understood that connecting their thoughts was actually obtainable, she realized that what she was asking from him was truly intimate—an experience that connected two beings on a level that could be nothing but.

He didn't take the request lightly, and she slowly realized why. It was a commitment of epic proportions being in the mind of someone else, especially someone that could live as long as they both could. She wasn't sure she was ready for the repercussions of the commitment, but knew they needed to make it if they were going to continue to search.

"I'm not sure what we will walk into, and I think it would be best if Zilla wasn't aware of your presence. If we run into her, or worse Erebos, I can cause a diversion while you search for your ring."

"You would be willing to do that for me?" His voice was awestruck, shaking his head as he looked at her. The rhythmic circles he was creating on her arms with his thumbs were soothing. She wondered if he was aware of the effect he was having on her. His dark eyes were hooded, and his nostrils flared ever so slightly. The scent of the rose oil she used on her skin that morning, and the musk rising from his, mixed together in a tender dance of longing. He was aware of it, just as much as she was. She breathed it in, and in that moment, she was willing to give him anything he asked.

"I would, Kadar. If you can make it so. I feel it gives us the best chance to face whatever's inside."

He slid his hands to the top of her shoulders and squeezed gently for emphasis. "You're sure this is what you want? To know each other's minds when open to one another, from any distance?"

"I do, Kadar."

Her choice of words made his breath catch, and her heart was swept up in the emotions of the moment. There was an energy that surrounded them that added to their intimacy; a magick she could feel but didn't recognize from her universe. It was as if her entire world had been blocked out, and he had slipped her into his.

"Once done, it can't be undone," he whispered.

Sevilla nodded and gave him a timid smile. The future had never been so clear to her before, especially since she was a creature that embodied the past. But meeting and getting to know this man was something she knew she was meant to do. Whatever this commitment meant, she needed to make it.

"Make it so, Kadar."

His hands slid up from her shoulders onto either side of her face. Her body tingled, anticipating the kiss she longed for. The opening of minds wouldn't require a kiss, and she was almost sure of it. But his intimate distance, and the tender way he cupped her face, confused her already aching body.

"You are the most beautiful woman I have ever known, Sevilla. You do me a great honor by this selfless act." His fingers were now at her temples, with the palms of his hands resting on her cheekbones. He tilted his head forward, so his forehead touched hers. Though the elements of an untamed mountainside surrounded them, she felt as if they were in a room behind closed doors. Alone.

"You're sure?" His breath tickled her lips.

"Yes. I'm sure."

He closed his eyes, and she did the same in turn, placing her hands on his waist for balance. She felt his body shift closer and heard the deep breath he pulled into his lungs as he prepared himself for the exchange. Her body tingled in anticipation. Placing her trust in someone like this wasn't done, not even with Ryker. She knew there would be no turning back. But she also knew there was a reason this man had found her, so she put her faith in the Universe for the first time since Ryker's death.

Soon there was a tickling in her mind, like an experience that she revisited over and over until she unraveled its meaning. Her mind filled with light, and she realized that the pictures forming there were not her own. She saw barefoot children playing in a dusty street and heard the haunting tones of a flute as the memory wedged fully in her mind.

Scents came to her next, roasted meats and savory spices made her mouth water. The picture changed, and they were in a large room with ornate furnishings. The man that stood before her was dressed in finery and had the look of someone who had lost touch with their soul. The light was gone from his eyes, and she knew somehow, as he fiddled with the large sapphire ring on his finger, that he would be making his final wish.

As the scenes filled her mind, she felt others leave. Memories that had served their purpose and were no longer necessary were being picked and pulled from her, like ripened berries from a bush. There was a humming, a buzzing, as if there was a hive of bees in her mind. Visions came faster, rolling through endless amounts of time and interactions with countless people. In every vision, the ring was present. Most of those who wore it no longer looked as though they had touch with their world.

The images flickering in her mind slowed, and a beautiful woman stood before her. Her smile lit the darkness, and the buzzing intensified. The voluptuous brunette with doe-like eyes reached to cup Sevilla's face, and she could no longer feel Kadar's hands in their place. She could smell the woman's perfume, a mix of jasmine and sage, and the chill of the metal as the ring touched her cheek. The woman said something in a lyrical language, something meaningful and heartfelt, and although Sevilla didn't understand the words the message was clear. She was saying thank you as well as goodbye. Her eyes filled with a love that took Sevilla's breath away. As tears started to fall from the woman's eyes, the buzzing came to a crescendo. When it was unbearable, it stopped, and Kadar spoke.

"Are you all right?"

Sevilla's eyes fluttered open, and she pulled her head back to see him more clearly. She was groggy, and the look of concern on his face was worrying her. Had the transfer taken place? And why were his eyes blue?

"Are you all right?"

His lips hadn't moved.

"Did you just say something?"

He smiled and pulled her into an embrace. His sigh of relief relaxed his shoulders, and she melted against his body.

"I did. I asked if you were all right, my jewel. I should have stopped sooner. I'm sorry."

She pulled back and looked at him, hands slipping from his waist to rub the outside of his arms. "What do you mean? Did something happen?"

He shook his head and smiled sheepishly. When he spoke again, she confirmed it was not aloud.

"Being in your mind was intoxicating. I stayed much longer than I needed to and shared more than I had intended."

His eyes were reverting back from a mesmerizing blue to smoky brown, and the look of concern creased his brow. She lifted a hand to his cheek to focus his attention on her; she wanted to be sure their connection was complete. Focusing on his aura, which reflected honesty and openness, allowed her mind to speak.

"I'm good, Kadar. I didn't mind the sharing."

A smile and a sigh was her answer. The connection was complete.

Relief flowed through his body and soothed his soul. She could feel it all, as it channeled to her from him, and could see the colors surround him as they calmed.

"I'm so glad. I worried it would be too much for you, but at the same time I couldn't stop. It feels amazing being able to talk to you like this. To have you share with me this way."

The intimacy was overwhelming, having him gaze at her as his voice tickled her mind. She could see what he meant about it being intoxicating. She could have easily stayed pulling at his thoughts for hours. Well, possibly not the last one. It looked as though she had been a lover and while Sevilla was curious about him, his past trysts were something she wasn't sure she wanted to know about.

A chuckle sounded in her head. *"Sorry, still with you."*

Her cheeks flushed. "So, you heard that?"

He smiled. *"Afraid so."* The tickle in her mind pulled across her thoughts and subsided. "I overstayed my welcome. I apologize." The sound of his rich voice was back, but Sevilla had to admit she rather enjoyed the intimacy of it being inside her head.

"I felt you leave. Like a warm blanket removed from my shoulders."

"I feel the emptiness as well. And as addictive as being in your head could be for me, I promise you I will never take advantage of it."

"So, we can control the amount of sharing?"

Kadar nodded. "When we have more time, we can practice technique. For now you will just have to trust my judgment that necessitates its use."

"I trust you, Kadar."

"I have great trust in you, Sevilla. Otherwise, I would have never done this."

"I understand why," she said, as she slipped her hands from his face. "Are there others you have connected to in the past?"

He shook his head slowly and cocked his head, as his eyes measured her reaction. "Not since my creation and not by choice. You are the first I have merged with freely."

Sevilla nodded, knowing that what he just shared was something they would need to unpack and investigate later. Why her and why now? Especially considering that they had just met. She cleared her throat and changed the subject, still unsure how she felt about this newfound information.

"So, I think the plan should be that you slip behind your veil, and we connect our thoughts before we get to the entry. Once I get us inside, we can start searching and see what we find."

"The ring shouldn't be hard to find once we are inside," Kadar said. "The pull is stronger. It is definitely here."

He leaned in and kissed her forehead gently, his warm lips staying long enough to let her body know they had been there but short enough not to overstay their welcome. The bristly feeling of his whiskers tickled her, branding her skin to crave only his touch. His next words were spoken in her mind.

"I'll follow you. Lead the way."

7

They didn't say much to each other on the short walk to the entrance to Erebos' home. There was no need. Since Kadar was back inside her mind, her thoughts as well as her feelings were his to examine. They were learning more about one another without words than she had ever done in the lengthiest of conversations.

The pathway narrowed alongside the mountain and then flared out enough for several people to stand comfortably. It was there where Sevilla remembered the doorway to be, she recognized ornate pillars that stood on either side of the platform. This was the place, at least it was the last time she had come here, which had been over a decade ago. She waved her hands along the stone surface, and the symbols for the opening lit as her hands passed them.

"The language looks like Sumerian," Kadar said. *"Similar to what we use in our culture."*

"It would be similar, although nothing that is recognized now, since the culture has disappeared. My sisters and I use it for our purposes, and most can't decipher it. Although, I suppose we didn't consider beings from the Multiverse coming here."

His chuckle warmed her. *"Considering you weren't aware of any, that isn't surprising."*

The rock inside the circle of symbols disappeared and opened up to a long hallway that went into the mountain at a slight angle. She walked inside a few steps, turned and paused until she felt Kadar's presence behind her. With a snap of her fingers she closed the opening, and the darkness covered them.

She raised energy between her palms, and a small glow of violet light brightened their path. She held the energy ball in front of her like a lantern and led the way.

"Your magick is as beautiful as you are," Kadar whispered in her mind. *"The color doesn't surprise me, knowing you as I do."*

"That's sweet of you, and entirely something no one else would have thought to say."

"It is the color of compassion and sensitivity. Is it not?" He sounded surprised, as if everyone thought about others by the color of their auras.

"It is," she laughed. *"But not everyone thinks as we do."*

"I have found that to be true as well. It saddens me that they cannot."

"Me too," she agreed. *"The world would be a much more pleasant place if people were more in tune with their true natures."*

The hallway opened up into a large room where several boxes were stacked, and herbs dried on strings tied to the wall. There was a small unlit fireplace in the corner. It would have brought them the first bit of warmth when entering the home, had it been lit.

"We might be in luck then," he said, as if she had spoken her thoughts aloud. It was going to take her some time to get used to him being in her thoughts.

"Perhaps. But it isn't always lit." She decided to take a risk and call out from here. Better to know what they were walking into. "Zilla? Are you here? It's Sevilla."

Her voice echoed in the rooms beyond them, but there was no response. She listened for activity, anything that would tell her that someone was there, but didn't hear a sound. She decided that the best place to start looking for a piece of jewelry would be Erebos's room.

"I already have a sense for it. It's calling me up the hallway to the left."

"I'll follow you then."

"Just passed the tapestry, the signal is stronger now."

Sevilla walked quickly up the hallway to the final door on the right. From the images he was sending her, she knew Kadar had already slipped inside. She creaked open the door and stepped in the room, noticing several things at once.

It was warm, and there was a large fire burning in the fireplace. Several scented candles were aflame, fragrant enough to know they had been burning for some time. The room was a complete mess, clothes strewn all over the floor, as if someone had tried everything on in their closet and not been satisfied with any of it. There was no sign of Zilla, but there was no doubt she was there. It was all of her clothing Sevilla was stepping over.

She heard a door squeak open, and just as the thought came to her to warn Kadar, her sister came out of the adjoining room that served as a bath. She was completely nude, except for the towel wrapped around her long ebony hair. As she looked up and saw Sevilla standing there, she jumped slightly raising her hand to her chest.

"Mother Goddess, Sevilla! You scared me to death! What are you doing here?"

Zilla continued walking, as she rubbed the towel a few times on her head and tossed it to the floor. She sauntered to the wardrobe on the other side of the room and rifled through what was left on the hangers. As Zilla stood there taking her sweet time looking for something to wear, the light from the flames danced on her alabaster skin. Sevilla heard an intake of breath.

"Kadar?"

"Yes?" The single word came out as a whisper.

"Well," Zilla continued haughtily. "Did you need something?"

"I...," Sevilla stammered.

"You need to turn your back, please."

There was a pause, followed by a single word laced with interest. *"Twins?"*

"I wanted to apologize. I thought more about our discussion in the woods the other day."

"Kadar?"

"Really?" Zilla turned with interest. Her breasts were no longer hidden by the door of the wardrobe and were just as perky and firm as Sevilla's. As if to draw attention to them, Zilla raised her hands to her head and fluffed her drying hair at its roots. The simple movement brought an internal groan from both Sevilla and Kadar but for two entirely different reasons.

"Identical?"

Her cheeks flared, and his chuckle warmed her in places she hadn't thought about in years. She was the spitting image of Sevilla for the most part, although their temperaments and taste in clothing had never matched. And Zilla had always been more sure of herself, which was precisely why she was prancing around naked. Something Sevilla would never do.

"Never?"

"Yes, it isn't fair for me to expect you to stay away from your home. No matter what has transpired between us."

She responded to Kadar with a snap. *"We can talk about all that later. Now turn your back please."* The situation was ridiculous, but she could hardly fault his curiosity.

He chuckled, and the sound covered her mind like rich chocolate.

Flustered, Sevilla picked up a red silk robe from the top of the pile on the floor and walked over to Zilla, placing herself between the jewelry covered dresser and the nude body of her sister. She didn't know where he was, but if her assumptions were right, she had just blocked his view.

"Yes, it really isn't fair," Zilla pouted. "Fate making me take Erebos to the Earth realm and staying away from our home."

"Kadar?"

"I can float, you know," he said playfully. Another chuckle, and then the press of his warm lips on her forehead. The fleeting caress brought a rush of familiar feelings but this time, he shared her mind. After a slight pause, his throaty voice soothed her. *"My apologies, Sevilla. It has*

been too long since I have seen such beauty. First I meet you and now to see your sister. I didn't mean to embarrass either of you. Forgive me, my jewel."

Zilla took the robe from Sevilla's hand and slid it on, tying it loosely at the waist. It did little more than draw attention to her pert nipples which now were poking the red fabric up and out. The tie hardly kept the garment closed, as she strode over to the nightstand and lifted up her hairbrush.

"Not sure you could ever embarrass Zilla," she said with a sigh.

"I am sensing she would be hard to fluster."

"That is putting it nicely."

She was happy to see Zilla didn't pay much attention to the dresser and went straight to the bed where she started brushing her hair. One hundred strokes, just as they all had done since they were little.

"I didn't have anything to do with Fate sending you away," Sevilla explained. "And if she did so, she must have had good reasons. I only wanted to say that for my part, as upset as I may be, I don't want you to think that I would ever expect you to stay away from your home."

"I have what I came for. I will wait for you outside the door."

"I won't be long."

"I know neither of you would banish me outright, but I have been left to deal with Erebos on my own since he isn't welcome back."

"Well, he is your boyfriend."

Sevilla still felt the connection with Kadar, but she could feel he had put some distance between them. She supposed it was as much privacy as he could warrant while remaining in the form they agreed upon.

Zilla blathered on. "I understand that, Villy. But he's different. Fate has made him different."

"In what way?" Sevilla couldn't help but be irritated. It was as it always had been. Everything Zilla.

"She erased his mind, and now he has no memory of this place or our life together. He doesn't even remember being attracted to me in the same way. It's like he is a completely different person."

"Perhaps it is time to let him go."

"But I love him," Zilla whispered. Tears brimmed and spilled over, trailing down her sister's face, but Sevilla looked back at her with a hardened heart. Now that she knew Kadar had found the ring, she could end the conversation she had never wanted to start.

"He was never a good fit, but we allowed him into the fold for you. He wasn't worthy of the power he wielded, but we gave it to him for you. He wasn't able to control his greedy hunger for power and killed the people we loved to obtain it. Zilla, he isn't right for you. Can't you see that?"

Her sister didn't respond. She merely bowed her head in defeat, holding the stilled hairbrush in her lap. Sevilla took the chance to have the final word. Maybe it would help.

"Destiny isn't always kind, but it is malevolent when unheeded. You have gone against her wishes before and have managed to come out unscathed. But this time Zilla, I'm not sure you will. And if I'm to be honest, I'm not sure he's worth it."

Sevilla turned and walked to the doorway, each step taking her further away from the last conversation she would have with her sister for some time. They both knew these would be the last things said between them, but neither one of them had any more to say. One last look back burned her sister's image in Sevilla's mind, an image of Zilla blowing her a kiss while sobs shook her delicate shoulders.

"Goodbye, Zilla," she said, her voice breaking with emotion. She was finally ready to move on and closed the door on her past, leaving it in the room with her weeping sister. She had finally come to terms with her loss and every step she took toward the outside world and Kadar, was a validation that she was heading in the right direction.

With warm tears tracking down her cheeks, she took slow and steady steps toward her new life. When she opened the door to the outside world, Kadar was waiting for her.

EPILOGUE

Sevilla and Kadar had made it back to her house long after night-fall. After saying a quick goodnight, each went to their respective bedrooms. They were both exhausted and neither of them needed to talk about what had happened, since they had spent the better part of the day in each other's minds.

She had slept later than normal and was surprised to see Kadar at the table when she entered the kitchen. He stood up and came to her side of the table, pulling the chair out for her and taking her hand in his to lead her to her seat. As she settled in it, he pushed it forward for her before taking his place across from her.

He had made breakfast for them, which wasn't as surprising as the small wrapped gift sitting next to the rose on her plate. She looked up at him, with curiosity in her mind, but he was only picking up on her physical cues. He hadn't been in her thoughts since Zilla's house. She found herself wishing she knew what he was thinking.

"What is this?" She couldn't help but be delighted. It had been some time since anyone had made her feel special. Even Ryker, as much as she loved him, had stopped the courting rituals long ago.

Kadar took a deep breath and pressed his palms together as if in prayer, with the sides of his pointer fingers pressed against his lips. He closed his eyes for a moment then dropped his hands to the table, reaching across with his palms up in invitation.

Sevilla reached out as well, taking his hand into hers and smiling to calm his fears. He was preparing to share something with her, something that was important to him. While she couldn't quite know what it was, she knew without a doubt that their relationship was about to change.

"What is it, Kadar? Is everything alright?"

His face beamed. Eyes that were once weary sparkled with a renewed life. "Everything is perfect," he said with a sigh. "It is all I could have wished for." He gave her fingertips a gentle squeeze and pulled his arms back, nodding his head at the wrapped package in front of her. "Open it," he whispered.

She pulled at the bow, created from a small scrap of ribbon he must have found in her fabric basket near the chess board. The paper wasn't paper at all, but a leaf from the sugar maple at the edge of her property. It was freshly picked and still flexible enough to wrap around the contents. When she removed the ribbon, the leaf unfurled, and she let out a gasp of surprise.

"I don't understand. Why would you give this to me?"

He shrugged his shoulders. "I trust you." His eyes registered concern, almost as if he was trying to determine if she was upset with the gift. She wasn't upset, as much as she was confused. The ring that drew him here that they had snuck into her sister's to find, was centered on her plate. She could tell by the power that pulsed from the silver encased sapphire that it was the ring that controlled him.

It was obvious to her that he hadn't made this decision lightly. And for him to place control over his destiny in her hands was incredibly brave. But what of the three wishes? How did he know she wouldn't use them if called upon? More importantly, how could she trust herself not to?

"Kadar, this is a huge responsibility. Are you sure you don't want to hide this somewhere else?"

He shook his head and smiled softly. His eyes reflecting patience and perhaps something more. "There isn't anywhere safer in this realm or the next."

"How could you possibly know?" She was disputing his claim, but deep down she knew the truth.

"The few times it has come into my control, I have hidden it. But it has always been found. I've seen into your heart and mind, Sevilla, and I know there are no safer hands for it to be in."

"Your faith in me is overwhelming."

He stood and walked over to her, kneeling beside her chair. She turned in her seat and allowed him to take her hands in his.

"You let me into your mind and trusted me with your secrets. This is nothing more than me sharing mine with you." He kissed the knuckles on each of her hands before looking up at her. "You are important to me in a way that I can't put words to."

"I feel the same." Sevilla glanced at the ring once more, marveling at its simplicity. How could a ring that could change lives or end them look so unremarkable? She looked at the man that was tied to it, the D'Jinn that was bound to serve the bearer, and knew that she would do anything to ensure that he would never have to call anyone "Master" again.

"Tell me what I need to do."

"Thank you, Sevilla. You could never know what this means."

"Show me," she said with a smile. "Come into my mind where we can discuss things openly."

"Ah, I thought you would never ask."

"That's more like it," she said with a sigh. She loved being connected to him in this way, to know how he felt about the words she said. *"What shall we talk about?"*

"Anything you would like, my sweet. Anything at all."

AUTHOR'S NOTE

Thank you for taking the time to read my words. I can't express how much it means to me.

The stories in this collection may seem different at first glance, but in my mind, connect back to the place where my journey began. A full circle that started originally with *Sea of Dreams*, now has the potential to continue with the next generation of characters. When I had finished the final book of the Power of Four series, I thought we were through with Wisteria, but my Muse apparently had other plans.

Wolf Of My Heart was my way of "getting back out there" after a long hiatus from writing, which is a nice way of saying crippling burnout. My challenge was to write a Fantasy novelette including mysterious panties for a fund-raising anthology I was part of. I had always thought it would be fun to write the "book" my character Brooke was reading in Book 1 of my Power of Four series. The reference to the cover art in *Sea of Dreams* is along the lines of a werewolf and an elf "getting it on" so when I mixed those two in with some lace panties, the story came pouring out.

Solstice In New York was the natural next book, since I left the first book with so many questions about the brother Sam left in charge when he abdicated his duties. I have been wanting to write a holiday story for a while, and this was the perfect fit since who doesn't love a winter wedding? This story also includes a cameo from Zilla, who is a prominent character in my Power of Four series.

I also decided to include *The Jinni's Wish* in the mix, especially since it has never been in print and ties into the series. This book was released as a reader magnet, and has only been included in an e-book bundle to date. It is a story about Zilla's sister, Sevilla, and is set in the time between the prequel, *Twist of Fate*, and the first book, *Sea Of Dreams*. What I loved about this story was making sense of the mysterious Kadar and giving Sevilla a story of her own that didn't necessarily include the sisters she was so close to. It also acts as an information bridge between the two books since it ties back to *Wolf of my Heart*, but also ahead to the 4 books in the Power of Four series.

If you liked these stories, I believe you would like Books 1-4, which are a little longer read and meant to be read in order, although Books 1-4 are standalone romances.

∞

The Fates couldn't maintain balance in the Universe...so they found four women who could.

Living one life, but destined for another, four women unravel the secrets of past mistakes armed with magick, friendship, and the love of men sent into their lives by Fate. Their first step will be harnessing the powers of Water, Air, Fire, and Earth. The second will be embracing changes to the futures they had planned for themselves.

A toxic force known as the Shadowman seeks a way to control the powers of the elements. It is only a matter of time before his evil spreads so widely that even their combined powers won't be enough to stop him from corrupting our world. All worlds.

He who controls the elements controls the balance. Without balance... well, you get the picture.

And so, it begins...

Power Of Four - Library 1 includes full versions of:
Twist of Fate (Dark Fantasy Prequel)
The Jinni's Wish (Fantasy with Romantic Elements Novelette)
Sea Of Dreams (Contemporary Fantasy Romance Book 1)

Power Of Four - Library 2 includes full versions of:
Winds of Change (Contemporary Fantasy Romance Book2)
Playing With Fire (Contemporary Fantasy Romance Book 3)
Heaven On Earth (Contemporary Fantasy Romance Book 4)

Interested? If so, head to the author's website at DAHenneman.com to download *Sea Of Dreams* for free! For those interested in learning more about the Magick and Mayhem of our favorite troublemaker, Zilla, you can follow her Facebook page at @EverythingZilla.

∞

If you like shorter stories, like the ones you just read, and adore Greek Mythology retellings like I do, my Goddesses In Love series might interest you.

History didn't always give them a happily-ever-after...it's time to change that.

Some characters were written to teach humanity a lesson; however, they weren't always given a fair chance to explain. Take Persephone, for instance. What if she needed some space from her mother and truly loved her dark, brooding lover? Or maybe Medusa actually fell for the sexy man who was ordered to kill her. Perhaps the brilliant Athena was aided by an unlikely source in order to win control of Athens from Poseidon's rule. And then there is Arachne...monster or misunderstood?

Each one of these stories has been reimagined giving these women a second chance at happiness. It is the least we can do, considering how long they have been seen in a less than flattering light. It's time they took back their power...it starts one story at a time.

Love For All Seasons
(Hecate and Hermes with Persephone and Hades)
A story about how Persephone and Hades REALLY met...

Medusa's Secret (Medusa and Perseus)
In Ancient Greece, sometimes death is only the beginning.

Athena's Challenge (Athena and Tiresias (Reese))
One is hiding their identity; the other is trying to understand theirs.

Web Of Lies (Arachne and Morpheus)
Controlling her curse just might be the easiest thing about their relationship...

The collection includes 4 complete novellas in a connected world, each with a reimagined ending to the myths they were born from.

Get your copy of *Pandora's Curse*, the prequel to this series, for free by going to DAHenneman.com and joining my newsletter!

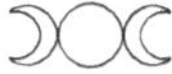

You can find more about all of my books on DAHenneman.com. The home page is where you will find my free book offers and latest shenanigans. If you liked this book, please consider signing up for my newsletter and learning more about my latest projects! I would love to have you along on my Journey!

ACKNOWLEDGMENTS

As always, thank you to my wonderful family. The past few months have been extremely challenging for me, and your patient support hasn't gone unnoticed.

To my content and line editor, Alexa Nussio, thank you so much for polishing my manuscript to a shine and recognizing the areas where I could dig a little deeper. Your suggestions are always spot on and make me a better writer. I am so glad to have you in my corner.

To my wonderful cover designer, Jen Sumeracki, a big thank you for helping me out with something I wanted to keep simple. We both know I can never keep it that way, and when I am wigging out, you are always a calming force in my life. Love you Sis.

To all of my Betas, CPs and BFFs you know who you are! Thank you so much for taking the time to read the draft, second draft, third draft, draft I didn't think I needed, and the final draft. You are the best support system a writer could ever hope for! Hugs to everyone!

And finally, to all of the amazing writers who have welcomed me with open arms into their colorful and diverse lives. Somehow you have made my world larger and smaller at the same time, which is a humbling experience. I am in awe of the creative force that now surrounds me.

Keep writing the words, the world needs them more now than ever and always remember to share the love! XO

AUTHOR BIO

While it hasn't always been part of her occupation, writing has always been part of DA Henneman's life. Poetry and song lyrics through teenage angst (no you won't get to read any of them), short stories in college classes (perhaps you will get to read some of them), and random marketing materials during her stint as a flower shop owner. Even with all of that writing in her life, ten chapters of a book stayed buried in her file cabinet until she closed her flower shop. The timing was finally right and the Power of Four series was born.

Most days she can be found on her blog posting about her writing journey. The best place to find her is at DAHenneman.com.

If you are interested in more books by this author, you can follow her on Goodreads or Bookbub. Be sure to check out the free offer for *Sea of Dreams* or *Love For All Seasons* wherever you find your books!

Happy Reading!